"Tell me, Lesley."

His voice was strong, demanding.

A heady, excited tingle coursed through her. *Heaven help me,* she thought frantically, *but I'm going to admit the truth.*

"Yes," she whispered. "Yes, I do feel it." His lips met hers again in a gentle but firm kiss. He cupped her neck with his warm hand to steady her while she laid her hand on his chest and felt his heartbeat.

She pulled away first, her breathing ragged.

"Why don't we go somewhere more comfortable?" Richard suggested, nodding toward the bedroom.

Lesley hesitated, wishing for one sweet moment that she could take Richard up on his offer.

"I'd love to," she whispered, "but I can't."

"Tell me why, Lesley," he asked quietly.

She took a deep breath and drew her hand away.

"Because I know what you're up to."

Dear Reader,

It's a brand-new year, and we at Silhouette Romance
have a brand-new lineup of dashing heroes, winsome
heroines and happy endings galore! Winter is the
perfect season to curl up and read—you provide the hot
cocoa, and we'll provide the good books!

We're proud to launch our new FABULOUS
FATHERS series this month with Diana Palmer's
Emmett. Each month, we'll feature a different hero in a
heartwarming story about fatherhood. *Emmett* is a
special book from a favorite author in more ways than
one—it's Diana Palmer's fiftieth Silhouette novel, and
it's part of the LONG, TALL TEXANS series, too!

This month, Stella Bagwell's HEARTLAND
HOLIDAYS trilogy is completed with *New Year's Baby*.
It's a truly emotional tale that brings the Gallagher
clan's story to a satisfying conclusion.

Rounding out the month, we have Geeta Kingsley's *The
Old-Fashioned Way*, Carolyn Monroe's *A Lovin'
Spoonful*, Jude Randal's *Northern Manhunt*, and an
inspiring romance from first-time Silhouette author
Jeanne Rose, entitled *Believing in Angels*.

In the months to come, watch for Silhouette Romance
titles by many of your favorite authors, including
Annette Broadrick, Elizabeth August and Marie
Ferrarella.

Here's to a sparkling New Year!

Anne Canadeo
Senior Editor
Silhouette Romance

NORTHERN MANHUNT
Jude Randal

Silhouette
R O M A N C E™
Published by Silhouette Books New York
America's Publisher of Contemporary Romance

With love to my three daughters,
Jessica, Rebecca and Allison

SILHOUETTE BOOKS
300 E. 42nd St., New York, N.Y. 10017

NORTHERN MANHUNT

Copyright © 1993 by Jude Wilner

ISBN: 0-373-08914-7

First Silhouette Books printing January 1993

Printed in the U.S.A.

Books by Jude Randal

Silhouette Romance

Just One of the Guys #889
Northern Manhunt #914

JUDE RANDAL

is a former travel agent whose wanderlust took her on more than twenty trips in six years. These journeys instilled in her a passion for romantic settings and happy endings, which she now weaves into romance novels.

Jude was born to British parents and lives in Calgary with three daughters and a cat.

NORTHERN MAN MONTHLY'S
HUNK OF THE MONTH

Name: Richard "Buck" Conway

Age: 29

Hair: Dark Brown

Eyes: Green

Height: 6′1″

Weight: 190 lbs.

Born and raised: Anchorage, Alaska

Profession: Pilot

Loves: Flying

Hates: Practical jokes

Mailing address: P.O. Box 000
　　　　　　　　　　Anchorage, Alaska
　　　　　　　　　　U.S.A.

Interested ladies can write to "Buck" at the address above or contact him directly through the magazine.

Chapter One

Lesley Lyndstrom's new boss wasn't at all what she'd expected. Just over five feet tall and well over two hundred pounds, Mae Barker had short, curly black hair, two chins and a full-figured body that she had somehow squeezed into a black knit dress. And at that moment she was laughing uproariously at her own remark concerning men and bathing suits and how the two, combined, had sent *Northern Man Monthly*'s sales skyrocketing during the magazine's second month on the newsstand.

Lesley had never met anyone even remotely like Mae before, and shifted from one foot to the other while the woman settled down and wiped a tear from her eye. It made her black mascara run and she grabbed a tissue from the pink box on the corner of her metal desk. At least Lesley assumed there was a desk beneath the piles of paper, file folders, miscellaneous letters and assorted glossy photographs. Covered the way it was, it was hard to tell.

Lesley ran her tongue over parched lips and tried to smile. But it had been a long trip from San Francisco to Anchorage, it was late in the day and she'd come to her new office straight from the airport. Anxious to begin her part-time job at *Northern Man Monthly,* she'd wanted to meet her new boss before heading out to a family friend's country boardinghouse where she'd be staying—as well as working as part-time housekeeper—for the next two months. Had she known that Mae was a little on the eccentric side, she would have gotten settled first and come into the office tomorrow when she was refreshed and alert.

Mae gave one final swipe at her make-up and hoisted herself from her groaning swivel chair. She opened her mouth to speak but before she could say anything, something just past Lesley's shoulder made her eyes light up.

"Speaking of someone I'd like to see in a fig leaf, there's my Bucky now," she muttered, studiously peering past Lesley and pursing magenta-glossed lips.

Lesley turned and looked through the glass walls of Mae's office to the tall, dark-haired man in jeans and a well-worn aviator jacket who stood chatting with the last remaining girl in the bullpen. If she'd been a little less tired, Lesley might have appreciated his lazy grace and the way he spoke with his eyes to the young woman by his side. He reached out and gently pushed a wheaten blond curl, the same shade as Lesley's poker straight hair, behind the girl's ear, his hand lingering just long enough to imbue the action with rank sensuality. Even through the glass, Lesley could tell that the girl was enchanted. If she fawned any harder, she'd be on her knees.

Lesley sighed quietly. Another good-looking man. Was there no end to them? Damned things were everywhere. She'd been hoping to get away from his sort when she'd left California and the broken relationship that had convinced her that although good-looking men were easier on the eyes, they were much harder on the psyche. It was that realization, backed up by years of watching her handsome older brother lead a string of girls in a merry dance, that had brought Lesley to the conclusion that a plain man was the only way to go.

And this man was definitely not plain.

"Come on, hon," Mae said, grabbing Lesley's arm, "I'll introduce you."

"No, really, I—"

But Mae was already out the door. "Buck! Hey Buck, you handsome devil you! How about a kiss for old Mae?"

The man immediately jumped to attention, turning his back to the nearest desk and raising a warning finger.

"Not in this lifetime. Keep your hands to yourself, lady."

While Mae and her target warily regarded each other, trying to see who would make the next move, Lesley idly wondered if Mae and Buck were representative of the people living in Alaska. Maybe she should have researched the state a little more thoroughly before committing herself to even this part-time job at *Northern Man Monthly*. She'd been looking forward to it, too, relishing the chance to be a reporter for the newly created publication that aimed to match single men from across Alaska with single women from across the country.

Lesley forced back the fleeting doubts, knowing that anything was better than being back in California, stuck in a dead-end secretarial position with no future. A thrill ran through her. She was aching to jump into this, her first newspaper job since completing her evening journalism courses. She could do this—she *wanted* to do this—and told herself to draw upon the same courage that had convinced her to abandon her well-paid position in a large accounting firm and sublet her San Francisco apartment. She'd ignored her father's advice that at age twenty-five she'd be wise to stay where she was, and had forged ahead to make a new and exciting life for herself with this offer of work in Alaska.

Yes, being offered the position at *Northern Man* had seemed like a dream come true—at the time . . .

"So," the man called Buck said smoothly, "you've been holding out on me, have you, Maesy?" He gave Lesley a leisurely once-over, then grinned. "What's your name, sweetheart?"

Lesley curbed her natural instinct to snarl something back, and favored Buck with an equally assessing going-over.

His jaw was dark from a day's growth while the rest of his face was tanned the color of toffee. The denim collar of his shirt peeked out from beneath his battered leather jacket, and he wore what looked to be a heavy bracelet of twisted gold around his wrist. His pale green eyes dared her to test him, as did the slow, sensuous smile that accentuated the tiny scar on his cheek just under his left eye. The scar intrigued Lesley, it made her wonder whether he'd gotten it from an angry bear or an outraged woman.

She remembered his remark and decided it must have been an outraged woman.

Sweetheart, she thought with disgust. Why was it that all good-looking men had to use such degrading, sexist terms? Doll, baby, sweetheart. Where would the world be if everyone, women included, talked that way?

"Just call me Toots, Hotcakes," Lesley said, straight-faced as she boldly extended her hand. He hesitated, looking her in the eye before slowly taking her hand in his and giving it a firm shake. She winked slyly and propped the same hand on her hip. "So, Bucky. The word is that you've got the greatest set of buns this side of the Great Divide. Care to turn around and give us a look?"

The silence was so thick, Lesley could have heard a pin drop in Wyoming. *Well, there goes that job,* she thought ruefully. *I wonder if they'll be needing another waitress in Alaska this summer.*

As she stood considering the advantages of slinging hash versus standing in the unemployment line, Mae's loud, sharp hoot pierced Lesley's thoughts, catching her off guard. She looked over to the woman who'd leaned her palms on her heavy thighs and was laughing herself silly. Even the girl at Buck's side snickered lowly before grabbing her purse and scampering from the office pink-cheeked. As for Buck, he stood perfectly still, his eyes sizing Lesley up with a stare so intense it made her squirm. As she had done, he was masking his expression to give nothing away, and Lesley had no idea what was going on in his head.

"Oh, my good Lord," Mae gasped, finally coming up for air. "I don't think I've laughed this hard since Old Man Marshall backed his truck up over the hydrant and flooded the basement. Whew!" she said, smiling through bleary eyes. "I'd say she got you good on that one, Buck."

He tilted his head in acknowledgment, allowing his gaze to leave the newcomer's face for a moment. "I think you're right, Mae," he admitted, turning his attention back to the blonde.

He smiled broadly. So, she was a spitfire, was she? Funny, but she didn't look the type, in her simple khaki outfit and practical shoes. Tall, for a woman, with straight, shoulder-length blond hair and cool blue eyes, she looked more like a Nordic ice princess in a winter festival parade than a get-down-and-get-nosy reporter. A woman of supreme self-confidence and breeding, he figured. Someone who didn't have much of a sense of humor. Still, for all her apparent composure, the newcomer appeared slightly concerned about his response, as though, having said what she had, she now wondered if she'd gone too far. Somehow he didn't think she made a habit of being forward with strangers.

Well, I guess there's only one way to find out.

With aching slowness, he turned his back to her, lifted the hem of his jacket, and shifted his weight to one leg to accentuate his jean-clad derriere. Several seconds later, he shifted feet again to give her all the time she needed to make a judgment call.

Lesley felt her heart drop. Mae's lusty wolf whistle turned into a series of heavy guffaws highlighted by a spirited round of applause. Lesley's heart dropped farther, if that was possible.

They're all crazy, she thought sharply. I've agreed to work for two months with a bunch of crazy people! Lesley ran her gaze down the length of Buck's body and back again, silently admiring the muscular build sheathed in faded denim. The fact was, he did have the nicest—

Lesley abruptly dragged her thoughts back to the matter at hand. Buck had by this time turned around and stood facing her. A confident smile creased his lips, telling her in no uncertain terms that he'd meant to embarrass her, and had enjoyed every minute.

"So, Toots," he said smoothly. "You call it. Do I, or do I not, have the nicest rear end you've ever seen? And please... be honest. I'm a glutton for flattery."

Lesley bit back a gasp of irritation and forced herself to appear disinterested. It wasn't easy. Despite her outward show of nonchalance, her insides were churning like white water, and all because of this man. He'd gotten under her skin amazingly fast, not only because he was better looking than ninety percent of the male population, but because he knew it and used that knowledge to his advantage. It showed in his face, his stance, even his eyes, which were at that moment admiring her with an insolent gaze that made her body tingle in acknowledgment.

"It's okay, I suppose," she said finally.

"Many thanks," he answered smoothly. "You can't *imagine* the pressure us sex symbols have to live with, wondering if we're the best this side of the Great Divide, and all." He gave a laughing Mae an exaggerated wink and turned back to Lesley. "But enough about my assets, Toots. It's your turn. Tell us about yourself. I'm assuming you're Mae's newest recruit in this ragtag operation of hers—"

"You got it," Mae butted in, crossing to the coffee machine just behind Lesley and pouring herself a cup. "This gal's our new interviewer. She's come all the way from California to help us out while Sylvia finishes her maternity leave, haven't you, honey?"

Lesley cast Mae a grateful smile. Maybe she wasn't so bad after all. A little rough around the edges, but at least she could take a joke.

"That's right," she agreed with a silent sigh of relief. "Excuse me. I don't mean to be rude, but I'm really tired. I think I'd like to get going and settle in if you don't mind."

"Oh sure, sure," Mae said brightly. "Your first assignment's not 'til Monday anyway. Take the next few days to get comfortable, and we'll see you bright and early then." She winked at Lesley. "I think you're going to fit in real well here. *Real* well."

She smiled broadly and returned to her glass office with her coffee, humming a Tammy Wynette song off-key under her breath.

Lesley stretched her aching neck and looked around the office that was empty except for herself and Buck.

"Do you need a ride somewhere?" he asked.

She glanced over, registering his confident grin, and turned to the large cork bulletin board by the coffee-maker.

"No, thanks," she answered, despite the fact that she had no transportation to the boardinghouse that sat some miles outside the city of Anchorage.

"Are you staying close by?"

"No."

"Rental car? Bus? A friend picking you up?" he persisted.

"No."

"Oooh," he said with an understanding nod of his head. "You're one of those."

"One of those what?"

"One of those don't-you-dare-lend-a-hand-to-help-me feminists out to make it to the top." He smiled suggestively. "Not that I mind women on top, you understand."

Lesley gave him a tired sigh. "Oh. You're one of those."

"One of those what?"

"One of those tedious little chauvinists who needs help getting his fat head through the door."

He cocked an eyebrow. "You've known a few?"

Lesley turned to face him, her brain instantly conjuring a vision of the insufferably arrogant male friend back in San Francisco who'd forbidden her to take this job. A very enlightening argument had followed his pious demands that she abandon her silly dreams of becoming a journalist and spend the summer in California with him. Against her will, she relived how he'd berated her ambition and tried to force her to forgo an opportunity that he knew meant the world to her. Lesley's indignation rose much as it had done two weeks ago when they'd had their showdown and she'd blasted him verbally. Never again, she'd vowed, would she put herself in a position where a man thought he could tell her how to run her life.

Lesley ran a hand through the hair at her temple, ired that her thoughts had strayed to the one topic she was trying so hard to forget, and embarrassed that she'd spoken of her irritation to a complete stranger. He must think she was one of the more peculiar females in the world, attacking his moral fiber without knowing a thing about him. Lesley cringed inwardly, sharply reminding herself that this man hardly deserved the brunt of her anger.

"Yes, I've met a few chauvinists in my time." She waved to the assorted photographs on the corkboard to change the subject. "These are very good. Did you take them?"

"Hell, no." He scanned the pictures of several men in various stages of dress and activity. "John's our photographer. I'm just a local bush pilot. I spend my summers flying sportsmen back and forth into the fishing camps. And, on occasion, when Mae needs an interview done or some photographs taken, I take John and whoever else is working at the time with me." He scanned her from top to toe and back again, smiling. "I guess that'll be you now."

And wasn't that just what she needed? Lesley thought with an irritating shiver of attraction. To spend time in some excruciatingly tiny plane with a man so obviously full of himself that she wanted to suggest he put out an entire issue of *Northern Man* advertising his own merits.

"Wouldn't it be Mae who goes with you?" she asked.

"Hell, no!" He laughed loudly. "I took her once, and that was enough for both of us. She spent the entire flight up trying to teach me how to fly the plane, and I spent the entire flight back filling her with cookies to keep her quiet."

Lesley smiled. "Yes, she does seem to be...uh..."

"Totally out of orbit? Perhaps even from another planet?"

"Unconventional," she corrected with another smile.

"Unconventional! You're being kind. If she had her way, every edition of the magazine would be a fig leaf special." He laughed, his deep voice filled with amusement. "I'd call that downright perverse! Yessir," he said with another chuckle, "it can be a real challenge keeping your clothes on when Mae's looking for men to fill the pages of her next issue."

Lesley had to laugh at the image that presented. As they'd stood talking, her earlier antagonism toward Buck had faded somewhat. Enough that she felt her shoulders relax. Her back still ached from the long hours on the plane, however, and the T-shirt she had on underneath her safari jacket was clinging to her travel-weary body. To make herself more comfortable, she slipped the jacket off and draped it over her arm, ignoring Buck's appreciative glance.

"Have you eaten yet?" he asked, casually leaning against a nearby desk.

"No, I haven't. But I am hungry, so if you'll excuse me ... ?"

"Let me take you to dinner," he said, reaching out and laying a hand on her arm when she would have walked past. "It'll give me a chance to show you a little of our Alaskan hospitality."

Lesley felt herself quicken at his touch, and immediately reined in her emotions. The last thing she needed was to fall for the first he-man she met in this land of men's men. She was here to work, not to start dating the moment she got off the plane. Besides, between her father, brother and latest romantic episode, she figured she'd had enough of the male species to last a lifetime. What she needed most now was some breathing space.

"Another time, maybe," she said vaguely, withdrawing her arm and moving toward her luggage, which she'd left by the door.

"Maybe." His tone was equally reserved, insinuating that it would be a long time before he made the offer again.

She stooped to pick up her flight bag, slung it over her shoulder and grabbed her matching portmanteau. It was heavier than she remembered, and she grunted with the effort.

"Need help?" Buck asked.

She looked over at him, immediately taking exception to his smug grin and the lazy way he'd leaned up against the desk with his arms crossed and one ankle hooked over the other.

"No thanks. I can handle it," she answered. "Don't put yourself out."

"Okay, I won't. Lord knows I wouldn't want to offend you. You might say something sharp and witty and hurt my unenlightened feelings."

Lesley couldn't cover her unladylike snort of reproach. "And I'll bet that happens every other day."

"More than you think."

This time Lesley laughed out loud. A sharp, crisp burst of disbelieving laughter, it echoed about the empty office.

"If I believed that, then I'd believe that pigs can fly," she said with a broad smile.

She met his stare and instantly felt her smile fade, for he was watching her with much more intensity than the moment dictated. She swallowed hard, unable to name the emotion that had chosen that moment to run rampant through her tired body and infuse it with a sudden surge of energy. Excitement? Fear? Sexual awareness?

She shook her head and tore her gaze and thoughts away from this man who had over the course of ten minutes caused her so many mixed emotions. He was brash, arrogant, smooth, self-confident and, worst of all, good-looking.

"I'm looking for a plain man," she reminded herself, horrified when she spoke the words aloud.

"A plain man?" Buck's look of honest surprise turned into one of delighted interest. "What for? You mean one in particular, or just *any* plain man?"

Lesley felt her face flush, something that hadn't happened since visiting Chippendales for her twenty-first birthday four years earlier. Her brain searched for a logical answer, but it was whacked out, like her body, and wouldn't cooperate.

"I'm tired of handsome men," she stated matter-of-factly. May as well go on the offensive, she figured. Save what very little face she still had left.

"You've known a few?"

"Yes, as a matter of fact, I have known a few."

She wasn't sure if he meant *known* in the biblical sense. If so, he'd probably laugh to learn how innocent she purposefully kept fledgling relationships. She ached to tell him that she dated constantly and had a little black book full of names to choose from, but outright lying went against the grain.

Sure, she dated, but very selectively. And not all that often, either. And heaven help her, but she never, ever took any male friends or acquaintances that she really liked to meet her family. Not after the first two unsuspecting souls she'd taken home for supper had been grilled by her father and brother as to where they were from, what they did for a living and where they thought their future lay. Not surprisingly, Lesley hadn't been asked for further dates. They'd been nice guys, too. People she would liked to have gotten to know better. Maybe these relationships wouldn't have led anywhere, but on the other hand, they might have. One never knew.

Lesley wondered what genetic flaw it was that so often infected otherwise healthy male specimens and caused them to turn overbearing and all-knowing. Macho and pigheaded. Insistent and nosy.

"Known, as in . . . ?" Buck asked.

Lesley snapped to. "Known as in I know, you know, he knows," she said bluntly. She could feel the beginning of a headache coming on and wanted desperately to sit down and relax. "Listen," she said, straining under the weight of her luggage. "I'd really love to stay and play word games with you, but I have to go. Don't bother seeing me out."

Buck tipped an imaginary hat her way, then cocked an ear to Mae's lusty voice as it called to him from within her office.

"Duty calls," he joked. "So long, Toots. See you around," he added, leaving Lesley to negotiate the heavy glass door into the second-floor hallway.

"Jerk," she muttered, cursing when the door closed on her ankle.

She fought the urge to look back, but couldn't resist one last peek. Through the glass she could see Buck waltzing toward Mae's office, his hands tucked into the back pockets of his faded jeans. He really did have a nice rear end, she thought idly. Not many men could fill out the seat of a pair of jeans with just the right amount of good honest flesh and still look masculine. As though he sensed what she was thinking, Buck stopped suddenly and turned, his eyes catching hers as a crooked, knowing smile creased his face.

Lesley flushed for the second time in four years. *Damn him!* He'd been counting on her gaping and sashayed across the patterned carpet to give her a thrill. He tilted his head toward her, grinned, then turned back to the office and Mae who was no doubt laughing herself sick again.

Lesley groaned in frustration, hiked up the flight bag that had slid down her arm and stomped along the hallway to the elevator. Coming to Alaska had been a mistake—she could feel it in her bones. No good was going to come of it, and for the first time since leaving San Francisco she wished herself back in her suburban apartment with a cup of her favorite herbal tea and a glossy magazine.

Buck watched the blonde storm off down the hall and laughed out loud as he entered Mae's cluttered office.

"What're you laughing at, Bucky?" she asked, leaning back in her chair with a curious smile and holding an oversize cinnamon bun.

"Nothing in particular, Maesy." He took a seat in the upholstered chair across from hers and rubbed the faded knee of his worn jeans. "Nothing in particular."

"You're not thinking of giving that girl a hard time while she's here, are you?"

Buck gave what he hoped was a suitably hurt look. "Who? *Me?*"

A solid hoot of laughter from Mae. "My good Lord, Buck. You are a devil, do you know that? That girl's different. You're never going to land her."

"You saying she's too good for me?"

"No," Mae answered quickly. "I'm saying she's too smart to fall for your tricks."

"Is she married?"

"Not that I know."

Buck nodded thoughtfully. "Then I guess we'll just have to wait and see, then, won't we?"

He rose and crossed to the dusty full-length window. Mae's office was situated on the second floor of a four-story building that was well-situated and close to downtown. Down below, late Thursday-afternoon traffic ebbed and flowed as people made their way home from work. And right below the office window, a cab pulled over to the curb.

Buck watched the cabdriver jump out and hurry over to the newcomer as she stood by her pile of luggage. She had her back toward the building as she pulled a piece of paper from her purse and handed it to the man. What was she saying? How difficult could it be to give the guy the name of her hotel and get going? And still they talked. Where the hell was she going? Buck wondered, fighting the urge to go downstairs and find out.

She finally climbed in the back seat of the cab, pulling her purse and flight bag in with her as she swung her long, shapely legs into the vehicle. The cabbie closed the door behind her and opened the trunk to load her luggage.

Buck watched the scenario with interest, his eyes narrowing as he willed the woman to look up to the window.

She did, frowning slightly when their eyes met. It seemed she was as leery of the sparks that had flown between them as he was, as unwilling, for reasons unknown to him, to acknowledge their intensity.

He watched the cab pull into traffic and disappear around a corner.

Next time, he promised silently. *I'll make sure there's a next time, and then we'll see if you get away so easily.*

Lesley lazily opened her eyes and gazed around the room, momentarily disoriented. Sunlight, warm and bright, streamed in through gauzy curtains making the yellow-and-blue flowered wallpaper appear golden. An antique bureau sat opposite the single brass bed, and two watercolors in old-fashioned frames hung on the wall.

Then, recalling her arrival at Conway House, she leaned into her feather pillows and stretched lazily. Last night's meeting with her father's wartime buddy, Bob Conway, had been extremely pleasant. She'd met him a few times before, but always when he'd been visiting her father in California, never on his own turf. She was pleased to find that he was even more likable when in familiar surroundings. A burly bear of a man, he exuded vitality and warmth, and made Lesley feel more like a daughter than a friend of the family. Unfortunately, fatigue had overtaken Lesley shortly after dinner and she'd had to cut their evening together short, apologizing for retiring early and promising to have a long talk with Bob the following day.

After showering in her small ensuite bathroom, Lesley dressed in a smart chambray shirtwaist and left her tiny bedroom under the eaves of the third floor.

Sighing appreciatively, she descended two flights of worn wooden stairs covered with faded Persian runners, the smell of aged pine and musty wallpaper filling her senses. When she reached the foyer, she turned right and entered the large informal lounge with its hardwood floors, strapping log walls and lava stone fireplace.

"Good morning, sleepyhead," a booming voice called out from the grouping of plaid sofas and chairs clustered around a hand-hewn twig coffee table.

"Good morning, yourself," she said, approaching Bob and taking a seat on one of the chairs. "It's a beautiful day. I woke with the sun."

He guffawed. "I doubt that," he said, shaking his head. "The sun rose about three-thirty this morning, darlin'. And it's now—" he checked his battered watch "—nine-thirty. By my calculations, I'd say you missed sunrise by six hours!"

Lesley wrinkled her nose. "Oops! I'd promise to do better tomorrow, but I don't think I want to get up that early."

Bob laughed, then leaned forward, resting his elbows on his knees. "Have I told you how much I appreciate your comin' to help out this summer?"

"Hmm, only six or eight times over supper last night."

"Well, I can't say it enough." He sat back and extended an arm along the low cushions of the sofa. "I'm not sure I could've kept the place open without you."

"Oh, come on. It can't be that hard to find a good housekeeper."

"Finding one isn't the problem," he admitted with a slight frown. "Gettin' one to stay—now *that's* hard." He caught Lesley's inquiring stare. "We've had three housekeepers here already this season and not one stayed longer'n four days."

"What happened to them?"

"Richard did." Bob sighed. "He can be...uh, well, hard to get along with." He shifted his considerable bulk and took a deep breath. "You have to understand Rich. He's a bit of a mother hen. D'you remember when Margaret died a couple years back?"

Lesley nodded. She'd never met Bob's wife but had heard through her father that she'd been a vivacious and outgoing woman with a heart of gold.

"Well, Rich took his mother's death pretty bad," Bob continued. "Blamed himself for not bein' here to help."

"I thought she died when you and she were on a backwoods trip?"

"She did. Appendicitis." He rubbed a finger along the knee of his jeans. "Richard couldn't have done anything even if he'd been with us. It all happened so fast." He sighed in remembrance. "Anyhow, now Rich's latched on to me, thinking that I'm gonna croak the minute his back's turned. Actually, he's become a real pest, tryin' to get me to sell the boardin' house an' all."

"He wants you to sell the boardinghouse!" Lesley said with honest surprise. She knew Bob well enough to know that this house and the wild land it sat on was his life. Had been for almost forty years. Although she'd never met Richard, she'd heard enough to know that he cared very much for both parents. Why would he want to disrupt his father's life even more than it had been? "Why would Richard want you to sell?"

Bob shifted uncomfortably in his seat, avoiding her eyes and generally acting like a little boy who'd been caught with his hand in the cookie jar. "Probably 'cause I had a, uh...tiny medical problem last year. Nothin' earth-shatterin', you understand," he added earnestly, "but enough to make him want me to sell up and move to California with him."

"I take it that you don't want to go?"

"No way," Bob said firmly. "Alaska's my home. This house was Margaret's idea all along. Sellin' out now would be like sellin' a part of her."

Lesley nodded sympathetically. "Why don't you just tell Richard how you feel, then?"

Bob snorted. "It's not that easy. He's...uh...." He rubbed his chin, which was covered with a day's gray growth. "A bit on the stubborn side."

"Well, I hope my being here isn't going to create a problem," Lesley said sincerely. "I can always get a room in a hotel if that would be better."

"No, no!" Bob jerked forward in his seat. "If you leave, I won't have a leg to stand on. I need you here to keep the place open. 'Sides," he said with a con-spiratorial wink, "I've never lost an argument to Rich yet. I'd hate to start now." He smiled at her over the coffee table. "Promise me that no matter what happens, you'll stay."

Lesley chuckled and raised her right hand. She felt there was more to this story than met the eye, but had already agreed to help with the housekeeping at Con-way House in return for room and board. She could hardly back out now. "I promise. No matter what happens, I'll stay for the two months we arranged."

"That's m'girl!" Bob stood up and winked again. "Listen. You stay here, and I'll go get us some coffee. Milk'n sugar?" he asked brightly.

"That would be nice," Lesley said, even though she rarely drank coffee.

"Be right back, darlin'."

He left, and Lesley took a moment to walk around the room. It was huge, and filled with red-and-black buffalo plaid sofas and chairs, a Navaho pattern rug and a twig card table set. On both sides of the fireplace, French doors with clear glass led to a covered porch, scattered with wicker chairs and spanning the length of the house. Past the encircling grassy field lay dense wilderness where towering birch and thick dark spruce trees mingled with heavy underbrush to create an overwhelming sea of green flecked with intermittent patches of white and yellow wildflowers.

Lesley was amazed at the lushness of the wilderness, considering Conway House was only fifteen minutes from Anchorage. A wonderful feeling of having come home washed over her, surprising since she'd been born and bred a city girl, and rarely had time to walk to a park.

A noise from behind interrupted her thoughts, and she turned to see Bob enter the room with two mugs of coffee, as promised.

"Good. You're still here," he said, as though he'd expected her to disappear in his absence. He put the mugs down on the coffee table and ran a hand through his shaggy gray hair. "I met up with Rich in the kitchen. He'll be right in."

They waited patiently, but there was no sign of the man. Bob ran his hand through his hair several more times, and shifted from foot to foot.

"Uh, maybe now's not the best time to tell you this," he blurted. "But I, uh, didn't exactly get a chance to tell Rich that you were comin' to help out this summer."

Lesley's inner radar flashed red alert. "Is that going to cause a problem?" *Not that I really want to know.*

"'Course not," Bob assured her. "It's just that, well . . . remember the other housekeepers I mentioned?"

She nodded.

"Well, he kind of made their lives, uh . . ."

"A living hell?" Lesley finished, only half joking.

"Oh, no, nothin' like that. Just . . . difficult. Actually, so difficult that the employment agency won't send anyone else out here for a job interview."

Lesley's eyebrows disappeared beneath her bangs. "Well, that's some recommendation."

"Oh, it sounds a whole lot worse'n it is," Bob assured her. "Rich is just a perfectionist like his mother, that's all. He expected too much from them women, an' I told him so. But deep down, underneath all that, he's okay."

Lesley highly doubted that. Still, it was obvious that Bob wanted this meeting between her and his son to go well, so she smiled understandingly and stood with her hands clasped before her as they waited for Richard to make an appearance.

Finally there came a shuffling sound from the foyer, followed by the heavy thump of boots hitting the tiled floor and then several muffled curses. Lesley bit the inside of her lip and wondered what kind of strapping caveman was about to appear around the corner. Judging from the man's colorful language and lead-heavy feet, she imagined him to be a four-hundred-pound wrestler who crushed beer cans with his bare hands and ate raw moose meat for breakfast.

She gave Bob a doubtful grin.

"It's okay, really. Just remember he's all bark and no bite," he said with a reassuring smile. "*C'mon, Rich. Put a move on.*"

"Yeah, yeah," the voice griped.

Bob slid a supportive arm along Lesley's shoulder and squeezed so hard, it forced her to cough.

And then a familiar figure emerged, filling the doorway and making Lesley jerk back.

"Okay, I'm here. Mind telling me what was so damned all-fired—"

Lesley felt her heart stop, then race. She flushed brightly, then paled, then flushed again.

No! It can't be. Life just doesn't work this way.

Although her feet felt bolted to the floor, she was somehow propelled forward.

"Lesley," Bob said proudly. "I'd like you meet my son, Richard. Rich, this is—"

"Toots!" Richard barked.

"Buck!" she squeaked back.

Chapter Two

"Toots?" Bob Conway echoed. A confused frown creased his brow as he looked from Lesley back to his son.

Richard tore his gaze from the woman before him, and turned to his father. "Mind telling me what's going on here, Dad?"

Bob scratched the back of his head and shrugged. "I'm not sure."

Richard propped his hands on his hips and glared at the tall blonde by his father's side. She didn't flinch but braced her shoulders and stared back at him through the same self-assured blue eyes he'd noticed the day before, in Mae's office.

"How about you tell me, then?" he demanded.

She smiled coyly. "Are you saying you don't know?"

Richard growled under his breath. This conversation was going nowhere fast, and he hated playing games as much as he hated black-fly bites in hard-to-scratch places. Think, Rich, my man, he told himself sternly. Why would Toots be standing here, in the middle of your house, on a Friday morning? Surely she wasn't expecting to...

"Aw, jeez." He groaned heavily. "You're not here to interview Dad for that stupid magazine of Mae's, are you?"

"Of course not." Her tone softened as she turned and smiled at the older man by her side. "Not that he wouldn't be a great addition."

Richard watched his father return her smile, and bit back a snide remark. These two shared something—that much was obvious. And they were standing together, opposite him, while he stood alone. There was something very significant about that....

A sudden thought hit him. "Aw, don't tell me you're here to interview *me.*"

"Guess again." Her stalling fueled Richard's ire, and he felt his frown darken.

Think harder, Rich, he told himself sharply. She's here for a reason, in your house, in Alaska, smiling at your father like a partner in some secret club. If she wasn't here in her capacity of reporter for the magazine, then what? The only other women who'd come near the house in the last month had been—

"Aw, jeez," he said, running a hand along the back of his neck. "You've come here to be a *maid.*"

Lesley stiffened, her eyes mocking and her voice cool as an arctic breeze. "As a matter of fact, I have come to help your father out. Do you have a problem with that?"

Richard noted her unflinching stare and the slight jutting of her chin, both clear indications that Toots was not a woman used to giving in. His own chin rose fractionally. As far as he was concerned, Toots could imagine herself Joan of Arc and Attila the Hun rolled into one. The fact remained that he'd gotten rid of the last three housekeeping hopefuls through subtle intimidation, and he'd get rid of this one.

He knew he'd have to work fast, since his father was champing at the bit to phone their regular summer guests and confirm their reservations. Without a cook or housekeeper, he'd had to hold back, but now that Toots had arrived, well, that changed everything.

Damn! He'd been hoping to have some time alone with his father to wear down his resistance and show him that moving to California was the best solution to their problem. Actually, he needed time to convince his father that there was a problem to begin with. And Toots, with her good cheer and offers to help, was definitely going to disrupt those plans. He needed her out of the house as soon as possible.

The mental picture of her struggling with her cases on the doorstep pleased him immensely. In fact, he might have been lost in thought for several minutes savoring the scene had his father's words not pierced his thoughts and brought him back to the real world.

"This is Lesley, Eric Lyndstrom's daughter. You 'member Eric, don't ya'?"

Richard nodded. How could he not remember? His father spoke of no one else when recounting his many war stories. He thought the world of the man, as well as of his daughter whom he'd met several times while visiting California.

"Well, Lesley's offered to help keep the boardin' house open this summer," Bob went on boldly. "She's come up for a part-time job with the magazine in town, but figures she'll still be able to help out 'round here.'' He gave her a bone-rattling hug. "She's a real sweetheart, aren't ya', darlin'?''

Richard watched Lesley bloom under the compliment, and wondered why his father could get away with calling her sweetheart when he couldn't. She'd wiped the floor with him for saying exactly that not twenty-four hours earlier. Women! What was to understand?

"Oh, she's a real gem, all right," he said smoothly.

His father didn't catch the undercurrent, but he could tell that Lesley had. Although she'd raised her hand to shield her nose from the smell of sweat and horse manure that clung to his clothes, the narrowing of her eyes told him that she'd read the sarcasm in his words and accepted his challenge. And as much as that confidence irritated him, Richard had to acknowledge a certain fascination with a woman who could stare him down. Clingy wallflowers looking for a meal ticket had never been his style, nor had the sultry model types who spent more time in the washroom fixing their make-up than sitting at the dinner table.

Not that he was looking for a woman. No, his life was complicated enough right now. What he didn't need was a relationship to distract him from his mission, namely, to get his father out of Alaska and safely settled in California. Another penetrating glance at Lesley convinced him that at any other time he'd be more than anxious to get to know this woman better. But not now. Not until he had the other matter settled.

The hall telephone rang at that moment, and Bob, looking relieved for the distraction, hurried off to answer it.

Richard waited until the man was out of earshot and turned to Lesley who was still holding a hand over her nose and mouth.

"What's wrong?" he asked, taking a step forward.

"Uh, nothing." She squinted and took two steps back. "Something smells bad, that's all."

"That'll be me."

"Oh," she answered with a lifting of one eyebrow.

"Not a very nice thing to say to someone you've just met, is it? *Hey, guy. You smell bad.*"

"I didn't say that!"

"You implied it."

She tilted her head and smiled behind her hand. "Well, maybe you do smell bad at that."

She took another step back and he took another step forward. "What's wrong? Can't stand the smell of dead rabbits?"

He relished the momentary look of horror that crossed Lesley's perfectly composed features. But it was momentary. Seconds later, it had disappeared and she was back to her old self, although her eyes did seem to be staring pretty intently at the red stains on the blue plaid of his flannel jacket. Richard was secretly pleased to have found a crack in the ice maiden's armor. Should he tell her, he wondered, that the red spots were really paint he'd splashed when painting the mailbox and that he smelled bad because he'd been cleaning out the barn? It would, after all, put her mind to rest and be the gentlemanly thing to do.

He allowed himself a sweeping glance, from Lesley's straight, shoulder-length hair to the shapely bare legs that showed beneath the hem of her simple blue dress. Another casual glance upward, with a meaningful pause at her bustline, and he met her pale blue eyes, which were at that moment watching him like a hawk.

Naaa, he thought wryly. *Let her squirm.*

"You and I need to talk," he said, raising his arms and stretching them above his head. He tried to ease the knot in his neck but it wouldn't be so easily dispelled. "I don't suppose you'd consider giving me a back rub, would you?"

"No, I would not! I'm surprised you'd even ask."

"So am I," he said thoughtfully. He lowered his arms and massaged his aching shoulders. "From what I've seen so far, I'd be surprised if you didn't carve my heart out from behind when I wasn't looking."

She huffed and went to walk past him, but his hand shot out and stopped her in her steps.

"I'm serious," he said, his voice brooking no argument. "We need to talk."

She yanked her forearm from his grasp and rubbed it as though she'd been stung. "You need to talk me into leaving here, you mean."

Damn! His father had already gotten to her. That was going to make his job harder. "No. I mean I have to tell you the way things *really* are, and you have to listen."

"Mr. Conway, this may come as a terrific surprise to you, but I don't *have* to do anything."

They stared each other down, neither giving an inch, until finally Richard cocked his head submissively.

"Okay, then. Please. Please sit down and allow me a chance to explain."

Lesley hesitated. He'd crossed his arms over his chest and stood with his feet apart in a typically arrogant male stance designed, no doubt, to intimidate. It had the opposite effect on Lesley, however, whose immediate reaction was to refuse to listen out of pique. She just as quickly dismissed the idea, reminding herself that he had been the first to back down. In her books that was pretty mature.

"Okay." She took a seat on one of the sofas. "Speak your piece."

Richard took a minute to remove his jacket, tossing it onto a closet doorknob in the foyer before sitting down on the sofa across from her. He grabbed the coffee cup closest to him and took a hefty swig. "This one must be Dad's," he said sharply. "It's loaded with sugar." The fact seemed to anger him. "When the *hell* is he going to learn?"

Lesley waited for Richard to say more, but he seemed lost in thought. She leaned back in the cushions, sipping her own coffee and crossing her legs as she smoothed out the narrow skirt of her dress. And still Richard remained silent, brooding over his coffee.

She took the opportunity to study him. Richard was tall, broad shouldered and ridiculously good-looking in a swarthy sort of way—and Lesley had been attracted to him the moment she'd caught sight of him through the glass walls of Mae's office. Thank goodness he'd turned out to be just as arrogant and self-assured as he looked. His natural insolence made it infinitely easier to remember that he epitomized the type of man she'd sworn to stay away from.

He was totally male, and exuded potent yet overwhelming masculine confidence. Lesley would, based on what she'd seen so far, say that Richard was a man who knew where he was going in life as well as how to get there. She couldn't imagine anything standing in his way, and for the first time since learning of the situation at the boardinghouse, Lesley wondered if Richard wouldn't get what he wanted this time, too.

Lesley sipped her coffee, alternately scanning the room and casting surreptitious glances Richard's way. Much of his confidence must come, she thought idly, from being so successful in his career. Bob had spoken over supper the night before of Richard's company, one of the fastest growing airline services on the West Coast. Heavily involved in year-round shipping and courier services out of California, Richard apparently left the operation of the company to his second-in-command during the summer months, flying back every few weeks to check on business while indulging his passion for northern bush piloting.

Then, it was back to California full-time for the winter, although Bob had mentioned that he could count on a visit from his only child during February's Fur Rendezvous. In return, Bob spent a small portion of the winter in California, staying with Richard in his Los Angeles apartment and touring to visit friends such as Lesley's father, Eric.

Lesley's thoughts came back to the present when Richard lifted his head and looked at her with determination.

"It would be better all around if you left right away," he said firmly.

She sighed. "You've already said that. And I've already told you that I'm not going."

"No wonder you're not married," he muttered.

"What's that got to do with anything?" Her eyes narrowed. "Besides, how do you know I'm not married?"

"Never mind."

Lesley sent him a scathing glare and took a hefty mouthful of coffee, cringing when its bitterness burned her throat. Her indignation was on the rise again, climbing with every second she spent in Richard's presence. Yet something kept her in her seat, some thrill of the fight, albeit a verbal one, that sent a certain excitement coursing down her spine.

She watched Richard rub his brow before leaning back on the high sofa cushions. To her irritation, she also noticed the long column of his tanned neck and the way his hair covered his shirt collar, and felt another compelling surge of attraction.

Another swig of coffee.

Richard sat back up. "I don't know how else to convince you to leave, other than to say that by staying, you put my father's life in jeopardy."

That got her attention. *"What?"* Not that she believed him, but still, what if he was telling the truth?

"Dad has—"

"Rich!" Bob's excited voice broke in. "Hey, Rich!" He appeared at the doorway of the lounge and waved his son over. "C'mon. We gotta go."

"Why?"

"Old Man Marshall's run his truck off the road. You gotta help pull it out." He smiled and gave Lesley a wave. "Sorry, darlin'. Won't be long."

"Don't worry about it," Lesley said, brushing aside his apology. "Richard and I were finished, anyway."

Richard growled and got up. "If you believe that, then I've got some Florida swampland I'd like to show you." He pointed to her. "You and I'll talk later. Count on it." He disappeared into the foyer, calling over his shoulder as he drew on his jacket and struggled with his boots. "Later, *Toots*."

"Save it, *Bucky.*"

"Count on it," he yelled back, his deep voice reverberating down the hall to the kitchen.

Lesley truly hated when someone else got the last word in. It reminded her of too many lost fights with her brother. In order not to dwell on the confrontation with Buck, she muttered some last word of her own and put the episode from her mind for the rest of the afternoon.

In her naiveté, Lesley thought it would be just that easy to dismiss Richard and the topic of her leaving. He did not return that afternoon, so it was only much later, after a delicious supper of baked salmon, cooked by Bob and eaten outside on the open porch, that Lesley realized the folly of such optimistic thinking.

She'd returned to her small but quaint third-floor bedroom, and stood scanning the forest from the long, curtained window she'd left open that morning. Because she had, the whole room smelled of fresh air and pine trees and wildflowers. Washing up quickly, she slipped from her dress into a pair of jeans and a light blue cotton sweater. A quick brush of her hair had it shining, and she pinned the sides back with two matching barrettes.

"There," she said, surveying the results in the bureau mirror. Being a city girl, she wasn't sure how to dress for a walk in the country, although according to what she'd read in a travel guide on Alaska, she was learning quickly.

She scanned her make-up in the mirror, wondering if it needed touching up. Not that she wore much to begin with, but somehow here in Alaska any make-up seemed inappropriate, surrounded as she was by nature's veil of purity and freshness. It filled her lungs and her mind, clearing out the big city cobwebs and somehow symbolizing Lesley's fresh start in life.

Deciding on just a touch of light lipstick, she leaned toward the mirror and parted her lips.

"Excuse me."

Lesley gasped and swung around, noisily dropping her lipstick as she twisted to face Richard. He stood in the bedroom doorway, dressed in clean, form-fitting jeans, a chambray shirt and his battered aviator jacket.

"I didn't mean to interrupt your, uh ... whatever," he said, "but I did knock first."

Lesley shrugged. "I was just making myself presentable." She tucked the lipstick away and looked at Richard. "So, what can I do for you?"

"We need to talk."

She sighed. "I told you earlier. We have nothing to talk about."

He took a step inside the room, and suddenly it seemed too small to hold them both. Lesley felt the nerves in the pit of her stomach skip, and knew that, much to her horror, she was feeling another pull of attraction to Richard.

"And I said we need to talk," he repeated smoothly.

Another step brought him into the room. With his hand on the door and his bulk blocking her only means of escape, Lesley had nowhere to go.

"Now, we can either talk outside," he added with a silkiness that unnerved her, "or we can talk here, in your room."

Lesley took mental inventory and came up two chairs short. The only place where they could sit and talk would be on the single bed.

"Outside," she said quickly.

"A wise choice."

Richard stood aside, and she strode past him with all the dignity she could muster. As she did, the aroma of his freshly washed skin mixed with outdoor freshness assailed her. She'd only met him yesterday yet already recognized the scent as uniquely his.

"So nice to see you do take a bath every now and then, Mr. Conway," she said, leading the way down the stairs. She heard him laugh deeply at her words, and felt her lips curve into a smile of her own.

Once outside, Richard led her to the back paddock that lay some distance from the house across an open, grassy field. There he stopped and hooked one booted foot on the bottom rail of the wooden fence. He'd grabbed a long length of grass from beside the house on the way out, and chewed thoughtfully on that while he and Lesley watched the horses contained by the corral. One pretty brown mare with a white spot on its nose came over and nuzzled Richard's hand. He obligingly pulled a carrot from his jacket pocket and let the horse grab it from his grip before stroking its velvety nose.

Lesley allowed Richard several moments to collect his thoughts. After all, it meant little to her what plan of attack he was hatching. She'd already given Bob her promise to stay, and she never went back on her word.

Richard kicked the ground several times with the toe of his boot, then looked back over the horses.

"It's important that you know why I'm asking you to leave," he began firmly.

Lesley bit the inside of her lip to stay quiet.

"You already know that my mother died unnecessarily while on a backwoods camping trip." His jaw hardened, and he drew a heavy breath. "Appendicitis, of all things. It all happened pretty quick, there

was nothing Dad could do. I might've been able to get
her out fast enough if I'd been here, but I was in Los
Angeles at the time." He kicked the ground again.
"That's where my company's head office is. An
emergency came up and I was called back on short
notice." Another terse sigh as his dark eyes scanned
the landscape. "If I'd had even the slightest hint that
there was going to be a problem here, I wouldn't have
gone. But everything seemed fine." His hands balled
into fists. "I was away for three stinking days, and
when I got back, she was dead."

Lesley swallowed hard. She'd never lost a parent,
never experienced the sort of grief and hurt that
Richard lived with every day. It was monumental, and
she felt her heart reach out.

"Anyway," he continued, "that was two years ago.
It's in the past. What I'm trying to do now is protect
the present and the future."

"By taking your father away from his home?"

He propped his arm on the top rail of the fence and
turned to face her. "I'm trying to get Dad to sell the
boardinghouse and move to California so I can take
care of him."

"I know. He explained all that to me this morning," Lesley admitted. "But he's lived here for over
forty years. He's an expert woodsman and guide.
Why, all of a sudden, is it so important that he
move?"

Richard released a deep, terse breath. "Because he
has a medical problem."

"He told me that, too. But he also said it was minor. Not life-threatening."

"Not—" Richard swore blackly. "His minor problem, Lesley, is diabetes. Not full-blown, but what they

call Type II. A mild case, but potentially life-threatening nonetheless.''

''Oh. I'm sorry to hear that. Still, why does that mean he can't stay in Alaska?''

Richard's jaw clenched. ''At the risk of sounding like his doctor, he's supposed to watch what he eats, stay away from sugar, keep his weight in line, etcetera, etcetera.''

Lesley assumed from Richard's frustration that Bob was doing none of these things.

''*And,*'' he went on forcefully, ''people with diabetes have to be extremely careful where their feet are concerned. The slightest infection can pose a serious threat. And last summer Dad got it in his head that he wanted to take a three-day trip into the back country, alone. As if that wasn't bad enough, while he was out there, he fell into the river, grazed his ankle and put the wrong antiseptic on it!''

His voice had risen so significantly that he was almost shouting. Lesley shrank back slightly, wishing she better understood if it was emotion or fact that was angering him. She hated to appear stupid, but she just didn't know enough about diabetes to see what Richard was getting at.

''You don't see, do you?'' he asked, correctly interpreting her silence.

''No, I don't.'' She propped her elbow on the top rail and gave him her full attention. ''You're saying that he got a bad scrape but that it could have been something much worse?''

''No. I'm saying that that little graze got infected and he almost lost his life, never mind his leg.''

Lesley gasped, and scanned Richard's face for any sign of exaggeration. There was none. He was dead serious. No *wonder* he was so anxious to get his father out of the boardinghouse and away from Alaska, she thought with sudden understanding. He'd nearly lost him in the same senseless way he'd lost his mother.

Lesley took a deep breath. "And even that bad experience wasn't enough to convince him to move?"

"Are you kidding?" Richard shook his head. "That old coot's as determined as ever to stay here. Says he's been taking treks like that one all his life and will continue to take them until the day he dies." He gave Lesley a stare so intense, it chilled her despite the gentle heat of the evening. "I'm just trying to postpone that day."

Oh, Lord, what do you say to a remark like that?

To buy time, she turned and watched the horses as they frolicked back and forth within the corral. Heavily shod feet stomped the hard-packed earth, raising little clouds of brown dust. A small gray jay landed on a fence post, cocked its head back and forth several times, then flew off. A lean black cat with three white paws emerged from the freshly painted barn, halfheartedly chased a fly, then sprawled out on the ground.

Lesley took it all in, then said softly, "I see your point, I really do."

"But?"

She forged ahead, her clear and steady voice belying her inner turmoil. She hated confrontations such as these, where she understood both points of view but was being forced to choose sides.

Another deep breath. "But I gave your father my word. I can't back out now. Not after he's been so good to me."

Richard's silence made Lesley uncomfortable. She could deal with his words, but his silence was unnerving.

Bob's earlier words came to her as she watched the barn cat swat at the fly. "Your father's told me he's looking for a live-in housekeeper to stay with him after I'm gone."

"We tried that. They're useless. We had three this past month alone, and none of them lasted. Hell, they didn't care about Dad's welfare. Payday. That was all they worried about."

Richard kicked the bottom rail with his boot, knowing that he was exaggerating, but not giving a damn. Lesley had to see that he meant business.

"Maybe you just haven't found the right person yet."

"The right person doesn't exist," he snapped. "Don't patronize me."

"I'm not," she snapped back. She took a deep breath and smoothed back her hair. When she spoke again, her resolve had returned. "You've only tried three housekeepers so far. There must be more than three people in all of Alaska who'd like to come and work for your father."

"We had the employment agency's best three."

Lesley gave a terse sigh, telling Richard without words that he was acting like a petulant child. He didn't care. What she thought was irrelevant.

"Okay," she said patiently. "What about running an ad in the newspaper? You'd probably get lots of answers that way."

Richard stared her down. "Trusting my father's life to some unknown off the street doesn't appeal to me," he said roughly. On this point, he felt very strongly.

"Even the credentials of the so-called housekeepers from the agency were debatable, but at least they'd been checked out."

Lesley met his heated gaze with a calm one of her own. "Are you sure you gave them every chance?"

A hot flash of anger coursed through Richard. "What the hell does *that* mean?"

"I'm simply wondering if in your heightened emotional state, you gave them every opportunity to fit in here."

Richard reined in his temper. Barely. "You're saying that *I'm* the reason they left."

Lesley looked back over to the barn, her silence confirming his insinuation.

"Well, you're *wrong*. I did not drive those housekeepers away." *I merely put them through their paces.*

He dragged a hand through his hair and studied the barn's fresh coat of red paint. It wasn't his fault the women had been unsuitable. Lesley hadn't met them. She hadn't seen how inadequately they'd handled someone as strong-willed as his father. If she had, she'd be sympathizing instead of fighting with him now.

"I'm sorry if you're angry with me," she said finally. "I'm not implying that you're out to hurt your father. In fact, I understand perfectly what you're trying to do." The mare returned to the fence, and she stroked its nose. "My first assignment after finishing my journalism courses was a series of articles on senior citizens. I was given the idea by my father, who has a lot of friends who are getting to the stage in their lives where they need taking care of."

"That only proves my point. Dad needs taking care of."

"Maybe, but there are different ways of taking care of people. Especially seniors."

She took a small step toward him, and he was immediately struck by the concern in her eyes. She didn't wear a lot of make-up like most of the women he knew, and that allowed her blue eyes to shine on their own.

"You see, what I found from working with the elderly, is that they need to feel independent," she continued. "One of their greatest fears is being put into a home and forgotten."

"You're way out of line, Lesley. I have no intention of forgetting my dad."

"I know that. But to your father, the loss of the boardinghouse would be symbolic. A sign that would make him feel that he was losing control of his life. You can see that, can't you?"

Richard couldn't see anything but Lesley's perfect features and tempting mouth.

"It's not the same," he insisted, tearing his gaze away from her face. "He'd be coming to live with me. We could buy a house together somewhere. Anywhere he wanted. Hell, he could have his pick. I'm not a poor man."

Lesley hesitated. "Still, that's not the point, is it? I mean, what would he *do* in California? How would he fill his time while you were at work, for example?"

"Any way he wanted to."

"But all his friends are here."

"He'll make new ones. Hell, he can visit your father twice a week for all I care. I want him close to me."

"Then move back to Alaska."

Richard hung his head and stared at the hard-packed ground between his feet. He'd considered all the alternatives a hundred times. Did he really appear so coldhearted that she couldn't see that?

"I can't," he said, lifting his gaze to hers. "I have a business to run. A big one. One that needs me to be there. In fact, I'm going to have to make several trips back to California this summer to keep things running smooth."

"Well, at least I'll be here until early September."

"Then what?" Richard was trying to stay cool, but it wasn't working. This topic was too close to his heart to be discussed practically. "Come September, I'm right back to square one, trusting his life to someone who doesn't really care. Besides, I've got a big expansion going through then. I won't be free to fly up here on the weekends. All you're doing, Lesley, is delaying the inevitable. Giving my dad false hope for staying here." He gave her a meaningful look. "Because I won't—and I repeat *won't*—allow him to stay another winter up here alone or with some incompetent."

Lesley saw unmistakable determination in Richard's eyes and felt a coldness settle over her. Was she doing the right thing, championing Bob's cause? Or was she, as Richard had so openly accused, leading Bob on unfairly? Perhaps—and she shivered at the thought—threatening his life?

She rubbed her forehead with her hand. How did she always end up in these situations? she wondered somewhat frantically. She'd only been in Alaska two days, and already she'd made an enemy of Richard.

She braced her shoulders, knowing what she had to do, but still dreading it.

"I'm sorry if you're angry with me," she repeated. "But my offer to your father stands. If he wants me to leave, he'll have to tell me himself."

Richard said nothing in return. He didn't need to. The undisguised contempt in his eyes said it all. Lesley felt another cold shiver, but stuck to her guns.

"I really am sorry," she said, reaching a hand out to him.

But he jerked his arm back sharply, his stare blank and unforgiving. "You'll excuse me if I don't invite you to the funeral."

Lesley's face instantly drained of color. Richard's remark had been unfair and cutting. Had she not understood the concern behind it, she would have been extremely angry.

"That's so unfair," she whispered.

"Is it?"

"Yes," she insisted. "Don't—"

"Save it, Toots," he ground out, and with one final icy glare, left the fence and stormed off toward the barn.

Lesley's heart dropped. What an auspicious start to the summer! Where in heaven's name could it go from here? she wondered, watching him disappear through a tall, narrow door. Her shoulders slumped as she turned herself and headed toward the big white clapboard house with its vibrant forest-green shutters.

Where, indeed . . .

She entered the house through the back door and the kitchen. It was her favorite room in the whole house, surprising, since she was one of the world's worst cooks and rated microwaved French toast as one of her finest culinary accomplishments.

Still, one didn't have to be a gourmet cook to appreciate the kitchen at Conway House. Six pressed-back chairs circled an immense pine table set with ruffled place mats. Honey-colored stained cupboards and paneling lined the walls. Glass-fronted bins held fresh fruit and vegetables, hanks of dried wallflowers hung from the beamed ceiling and simple muslin curtains billowed at the open window.

Lesley plugged in the kettle to make herself a cup of tea and allowed her mind to wander as she puttered around, arranging the antique canisters and collectibles on the counter and fussing in the small linen cupboard while the water boiled. A cup of rose hip tea in her hand, she took a seat at the table just as Bob barged into the room.

"Good, I found you," he said, grabbing a mug from the hook under a cupboard and pouring himself a large mug of coffee from the percolator. He brought it over to the table and straddled a chair that groaned beneath his weight.

"Did you think I'd left?" she teased, watching with concern as he spooned a large dose of sugar into his cup. Now that she knew about his diabetes, she could understand Richard's concerns regarding his health. It was obvious that Bob wasn't taking his doctor's advice to heart. Maybe Richard was right. Maybe Bob did need closer watching after all. Silently she made a note to visit a grocery store as soon as possible and get him some artificial sweetener for his coffee.

"No, darlin'," he said with a hearty laugh. "I didn't think you'd left. You're made of stronger stuff'n that." He laughed again. "No daughter of Wild Eric Lyndstrom could be anythin' but a trooper."

Lesley smiled at the reference to her father and sipped her tea. She'd always found other people's conception of the man fascinating. For example, Bob Conway saw him as the greatest war hero who'd ever lived, no doubt recalling their adventures through rose-colored glasses. And her mother saw Eric Lyndstrom as a woman's dream come true, rewarding his loving but high-handed ways with a lifetime of devotion. And then there was Lesley's older brother who considered his father's constant meddling a good-natured, if sometimes annoying, attempt at communication.

Funny how only Lesley saw her father's manipulative side. Oh, she loved him, but that didn't mean she wouldn't like him to be a little more…bending. More open to suggestions. A little less bossy. A little less macho, if the term could be applied to a sixty-eight-year-old man.

She remembered how he'd managed to railroad her into secretarial school when all she'd really wanted to do was become a journalist, and mourned the years she'd wasted typing when she should have been out following her dream. Still, he was her father, and he'd done what he thought best. She could hardly fault him for caring.

"So, how're you'n Rich getting along?" Bob asked, interrupting Lesley's daydream.

She took a sip of tea and shrugged. "As well as can be expected, I guess. He's determined to get you to California any way he can. To him, my helping out this summer is just postponing the inevitable."

"No, no. Your bein' here is gonna give me the time to find a housekeeper he likes. He said he'd leave me alone if I found a good one. All's I need is someone to cook and clean. I still got my marbles. I don't need no baby-sitter.''

Lesley sat back in her chair. So she'd been right. Bob *was* concerned about losing his independence. What a shame that he was being confronted with such premature worries when from what she could see, he had many good years of self-sufficiency left. It was a pity Richard was too emotionally involved to see that.

She looked back to Bob as he leaned forward and began regaling her with yet another war story involving himself and Wild Eric Lyndstrom.

Oh, well, she thought, settling in for a long one. Think of your stay here as being strapped to a raft. You're already in the white water. May as well shoot the rapids and see where they take you.

Chapter Three

Three days later, Richard sat on the front porch of Conway House contemplating the similarities between Lesley and the tenacious tree stump by the porch steps. He couldn't seem to get rid of either. Shrugging, he rose and entered the house to look for Lesley, something telling him she'd be in the kitchen.

The smell wafting through the arched doorway into the hall confirmed it. Burned something. He hoped it was not burned breakfast.

Lesley stood over the stove, wrestling with a spatula and a shallow fry pan. Her lips were pursed, and her eyebrows were drawn together in concentration. She seemed frazzled, hot and breathtakingly pretty.

"Dammit, dammit, dammit," she muttered under her breath. "I'm giving you one more chance, and that's it," she told the blackened blob in the pan. She picked it up with her tongs and carried it over to the garbage can. "There," she snapped, tossing it in and allowing the lid to bang closed. "No evidence."

Richard choked back a laugh and watched her wipe out the pan and fiddle with the stove controls. Three days had passed since their talk at the corral, time away that he'd used to come to grips with Lesley and her militant loyalty toward his father. Although it still bugged him and threatened to make his job harder, he honestly regretted the harsh words he'd dealt her. He'd had no right to come down on Lesley that way. She was simply an innocent bystander who'd stumbled into the middle of a family feud. Confronted by two opposing opinions, and understanding both, it was honor, not obstinacy, that was driving her to keep her promise to his father. Richard could understand that, for he was a man of his word and often had to follow through on promises that he wished he'd never made.

He watched Lesley pause to sip from a glass of iced tea before shoving her shirt into her pants waistband with a sharp jab of her hand. This was a different side of her, frazzled and frustrated, a complete contrast to her original frosty appeal. Although he found her regal demeanor, insolent stares and cool tones when verbally sparring a distinct turn-on, he liked seeing this side of her, too. There was fire under that ice, and he meant to taste of it.

Which brought him to Plan B: the removal of one Lesley Lyndstrom from Conway House—and his father's life—through the time-honored method of sweet-talking. Plan A, bullying, hadn't worked, but he was sure this would. Not that he was an expert on the subject, but he had, over the years, enjoyed a certain level of success in convincing women that they wanted what he wanted.

Of course, most of those women had started out liking him.

His brow furrowed. As far as he knew, Lesley despised him. And why not? He'd given her good reason. Damn! Why hadn't he kept his cool when trying to talk her into leaving that first day? She was a burr under his saddle, and Lord help him but he just didn't think clearly when she was around. Still, there was more than one way to skin a cat.

He ran a hand along the back of his neck and straightened his shirt collar before entering the kitchen with a hundred-watt smile.

"Morning, Toots!" he greeted. "How's it going?"

Lesley jumped at the sound of his voice and held a hand over her heart. "Good grief, you scared me half to death."

"What's the matter?" he said smoothly, coming to lean on the island's countertop, opposite her. "Figured I'd dropped off the face of the earth?"

She pushed a stray lock of shining hair behind her headband with the back of her hand. "*Hoping* you had, more like it," she muttered, her eyes on the bowl of pancake mixture she was whipping to a froth.

Richard laughed loudly, realizing how much he'd missed Lesley's sharp tongue and quick wit these past three days. Her impertinence was a breath of fresh air, and it kept him on his toes.

"So what are you cooking there, anyway?"

"I'm practicing crepes," she said, pursing her lips as she poured more batter into the shallow pan.

"First time?"

"*Yes*, it's the first time." Her face was flushed although it wasn't hot in the kitchen. She laid the back of her hand on her cheek. "What's it to you?"

Richard bit back a grin. Julia Child she was not. Maybe Plan B wouldn't be necessary after all. If Lesley's cooking was as bad as all that, it could conceivably kill off the guests due to arrive shortly and solve the problem of keeping the boardinghouse open that way.

"I've never had crepes. Are they any good?"

"Would you like to try one?" she asked dryly, pointing to the uncooperative mass in her pan.

Richard craned his neck and stared down at it. "Is it something *real* men eat?" He smiled up at her. "Or is it in the same category as quiche?"

"Real men," Lesley scoffed, flipping the watery pancake over. It landed in a runny lump in the corner of the pan and lay there as though it had been shot. "Oh, I give *up!*" She carried the pan over to the garbage can and shot the crepe into the bin. "It's toast from now on."

"You could always nibble on these," Richard said when she'd returned to the counter. He pulled a pretty ribbon-tied box of chocolates from his pocket and pushed them toward her.

She stared at the box, looked him in the eye, then nudged the pink ribbon with her tongs.

"What are they?"

"Chocolates," he said with a grin. "Don't you like chocolates?"

She didn't answer right away, but watched him through narrowed eyes. "Why?"

"Why am I giving you chocolates?" She nodded. "To say I'm sorry for our conversation the other night. I said some pretty rude things. I get a bit emotional where Dad's concerned."

She shrugged. "That's okay. I understand."

"Thanks." He smiled hopefully. "So I'm forgiven?"

She watched him for several long moments during which he kept his expression suitably penitent, his smile weak and his eyes hopeful. Finally she huffed, sent him a look that said she was not completely convinced of his sincerity and picked up the peace offering.

"What kind are they?" she asked, gently shaking the box.

"My personal favorite. Maraschino cherries."

She growled, then smiled. "Boy, you're lucky. Cherries are my favorite, too. Thank you very much."

"I was hoping you'd offer me one."

"Not likely, but no harm in asking." She grinned and tucked the box into the pocket of her apron, then set to work cleaning up her mess.

His mother's apron, Richard thought with a jolt. Lesley must have found it at the back of the linen cupboard and put it on to keep her clothes clean. One of his mother's favorites. It was enough to make him remember the task at hand.

"So how are you fitting in?" he asked casually. "I hear you offered to help with the cooking as well as the cleaning around here. It sounds like Dad's working you pretty hard."

"Not at all," she answered, carrying her utensils to the sink beneath the open window. "I'm only helping with the meals until he finds a proper cook. Hopefully that'll be before the guests arrive." She pulled a face. "You might not have noticed, but I'm not the world's best."

"Has he phoned any of the guests yet?"

"Mmm-hmm. Last night, in fact. Only one couple can't make it after all. But the rest can. Not that there's many, but it should keep this place lively until the end of August."

Richard had to force himself to smile. "Good, good." He strode over to where Lesley stood washing the dishes, her hands encased in yellow rubber gloves.

She glanced over to him. "So where did you get to this time?"

He shrugged. "Here and there. Took a planeload of city slickers down to Afognak Island to fish for red salmon. It was a good group," he added, grinning. "Only four came close to drowning this time."

He slipped off his leather jacket and tossed it onto the counter as Lesley peeled off her gloves and threw them in the cupboard underneath the sink. She turned, and Richard saw his chance. Quickly covering the distance between them, he propped his hands on the counter, one on each side of her hips.

"So tell me, Toots, what are your plans for today?" he asked, scanning her face. She was more attractive than he remembered, and smelled fresh and sweet. Her skin was smooth and glowing with health, her cheeks pink and feminine.

A suspicious frown marred her brow. "Just a little housework before going in to work this afternoon. But I—"

"Tell you what, then," he cut in smoothly. He slid the fabric band from her head and ran a hand through hair that felt like silk. "What say after breakfast you and I go for a drive to my cabin? It'll give you a taste of the true outdoors. Show you how northern men really live."

Lesley hesitated. "I'm not sure. Your father—"

"Is out for the day. At least until supper."

"Oh. Right." She hesitated again, her gaze swinging back and forth across the expanse of his chest.

"It'd be good research," he said, baiting the hook. "You never know when you might be asked to write an article about the Last Frontier."

Lesley hesitated as she looked deep into Richard's eyes. Think this through, she told herself firmly. You're a reasonably intelligent girl—figure it out. And she was sure there was something to figure out. No man could be so scathing and cold one day and so charmingly humble the next.

Lesley's eyes darted back to Richard, who was patiently waiting for her answer to his invitation, as she tried to read his thoughts. If there was one thing she'd learned over the years, it was that there was none of God's creatures more conniving than a man who wanted something. And Richard wanted Lesley out of his father's house. The only thing she didn't know was how he intended to go about that, although she already knew enough about Buck Conway to sense that he'd try almost anything.

So we're playing dirty, are we, Mr. Conway? Lesley smiled coyly. *Well, two can play that game.*

She wasn't sure where all this was leading but she was game to find out. "Your cabin," she repeated with seeming interest. "Well, I'm flattered that you'd take the time to show me it, but really, I don't want to bother you."

"It's no bother. Trust me."

"Oh, I do," she lied smoothly. *Like a snake in the grass.*

She nibbled her lower lip, trying her best to appear coquettish when all she really wanted to do was slap her hands on Richard's chest and push past him with a knowing sneer. To draw out the moment and make him wait for an answer, she glanced down to his chest, irritation warming her cheeks when the sight of his muscles straining against the fabric of his shirt sent her senses soaring. Lesley immediately cursed his ability to physically attract her, and she took a deep breath. He smelled totally male, freshly showered and musky, with a natural scent that drew her to him instinctively.

Remember the game plan, Les. Don't be swayed by a pretty face. Lord knows you've fallen for enough of those in your time.

Dragging her thoughts back to Richard, she forced a smile and met his gaze. "Well, if you're sure it's no bother, I'd love to see your cabin," she said, surprised when her voice sounded calm and collected.

"Great. It's settled," he said, stepping back. "I've got to check on the horses. Give me half an hour, and we'll go."

He smiled again, gently chucked her chin with his knuckles, and left the kitchen through the back mudroom. Seconds later, he was crossing the open field on his way to the barn, his step light and a song on his lips.

Lesley stared out the kitchen window at Richard's retreating figure, her lips pressed into a fine line and her thoughts scrambling around in her brain. They fell in a jumble and left her without a conclusive answer as to Richard's plan of attack, so she watched him disappear behind the barn door and turned her attention to the kitchen and the mundane.

Her breakfast plate sat on the counter, empty except for two cold bread crusts. Funny, but she still hated crusts. Five years after moving out of her parents' house, and she still tried to eat them because her mother said she should. Lesley recalled the many times when as a child she'd refused to eat her dinner and had been subjected to one of her mother's profound speeches on life, waste and the long-term benefits of eating liver. And then, if Lesley still refused to eat, out would come the smile. Not just *a* smile, but *the* smile. Wistful, hopeful and just short of overwhelming, it was always enough to get Lesley to eat anything put down before her....

Lesley's glare hardened as she finally realized where Richard was going with this. He was trying to sweet-talk her into leaving his father's house! Anger suffused her face with heat and caused her breath to stick in her chest. What incredible gall! A few kisses, a couple of romantic times together and voilà! Lesley would be so besotted with Richard that she'd be dying to do whatever he wanted her to—including moving out of Conway House. In fact, he'd already started, waltzing in today like some northern Valentino, spewing sweetness and light and making her feel as if she was the only woman on earth who mattered.

Not that she'd fallen for it, but it still bugged her to think that he'd try such a low trick.

He obviously doesn't know who he's dealing with.

"Well, you're about to find out," she muttered darkly, quickly planning her own offensive as she cleaned up the kitchen in record time and ran upstairs to change. There was a lesson that needed teaching here, and there was no time like the present. After freshening up, she changed into her best pair of chambray jeans and her light blue cotton sweater. She left her hair free of restraints and brushed it until it crackled. Then she went down to the lounge, forcing the determined frown from her face and casually flipping through a fishing magazine while she waited for the almighty Richard Conway to finish his chores.

He returned ten minutes later. "Ready?" he asked, tucking his shirt into his waistband.

She rose from the sofa and nodded. "You bet I'm ready."

"Good. Let's go."

As they drove, Richard explained how the cabin was five minutes away as the crow flew, but eight by truck. It sat on the same piece of heavily forested property as Conway House and belonged to his father who visited the cabin every now and then for old times' sake. Richard's truck quickly covered the ride down the driveway of Conway House before veering along a dirt side road so filled with potholes that Lesley wished she'd brought a pillow to sit on despite the luxurious upholstery of the truck.

Richard brought the vehicle to a stop with a jerk that would have sent Lesley through the windshield had it not been for her seat belt, then jumped out and came to open her door.

"Thanks," she said wryly, accepting his hand as she stepped down. Her legs wobbled beneath her, and she was glad when he took her elbow to help her up the gravel path to the porch steps.

His cabin, a single-story log structure with a red asphalt roof, was nothing if not primitive, she thought, as he escorted her up the stairs. The tour of the outside took approximately two and a half minutes, and that included time to stop and peek in the small curtainless windows as well as stare out over the surrounding grassy field that separated the cabin from the usual scrub and thick forest of Bob's property.

When they'd circled back to the front door, Richard smiled contentedly and propped his hands on his hips.

"Want to see inside now?" he asked.

Lesley shook her head. "Actually, I'd like to sit out here for a while, if that's all right."

"Sure." He ushered her to one of two wooden chairs with homemade cushions that had seen better days. "Peaceful, isn't it?" he said, sitting down in the one beside hers.

"It sure is. Why, it's so quiet—oh my *God!*" Lesley squawked, for at that moment, from behind the cabin, there came the loudest barking she'd ever heard followed directly by a massive ball of silver-brown fur that bounced up the porch steps and skittered back and forth, claws clicking noisily against the wood porch in a welcoming frenzy.

"Hi ya', Wolf," Richard said, roughly rubbing the dog's head. The animal jounced around a bit more before finally standing still, panting heavily and showing Lesley a few more teeth than she cared to see. "There's a good boy. Sit down," Richard commanded gently. The dog did, licking his master's hand and whining appreciatively.

Lesley sat ramrod still, afraid to move and barely breathing. Her mother's allergies had prevented the family from having pets when she'd been young; her only real experience with animals had been a dog bite she'd received when visiting friends as a child. "Why did you name him that?" she asked, watching the dog with hawk eyes.

"Because he's half wolf, half husky, aren't ya' boy?" He scratched the dog's chin and leaned back in his creaky chair. "He stays with me at the house in Los Angeles during the winter, but he's happiest here."

Lesley forced her body to relax. She'd heard that animals could sense fear. If that was the case, then Wolf was probably sizing her up for a snack right now.

"So, Richard," she said in what she hoped was a casual voice. "This is where you live when you're in Alaska."

"Most of the time. Sometimes I stay at Dad's house, if the mood strikes me." His gaze wandered past the porch railings to the vast enveloping green. "But this is where I'm really at home. It's so simple. No lights, no noise." Wolf chose that moment to growl deep in his throat and take off like a bolt of lightning, his loud barking permeating the warm summer air and following him across the field into the underbrush.

Richard shot Lesley a wry grin. "Well, almost no noise."

She relaxed her shoulders, which had tensed up at the dog's frantic departure, and nestled into her seat.

"I live close to downtown myself, so I know what life in the big city is like," she said casually. "And this is the farthest thing from it." She let her eyes feast on the lush green of their surroundings, and breathed deeply of the pine-scented air. It was heavy with the heat of the day and surrounded her like a favorite blanket. She smiled broadly. "The more I see of Alaska, the more I understand why you love it here," she said sincerely.

He seemed honestly surprised. "You mean that?"

"Sure. It makes life back home seem so... hectic."

He leaned back and crossed one leg over the other knee. "What really made you come to Alaska?" he asked quietly.

Lesley stopped short. Richard already knew that the job at *Northern Man Monthly* had brought her north. What more could she add? Fleetingly, she questioned the motive behind his question, hating her suspicion but unable to ignore the little voice in her brain that told her to keep her defenses in place.

A familiar face flashed past her eyes as she relived the last time she'd let her guard down and trusted a man. A good-looking man. A good-looking man with a very high opinion of himself and a slightly arrogant manner that had turned very arrogant when Lesley had refused to be bullied into giving up her dream of becoming a journalist. After the heated argument following her refusal, there was no chance of them getting back together. Lesley wouldn't have him if he came begging on his knees, and no doubt he felt the same way about her.

"I figured as much," Richard said wryly. "You had a fight with your boyfriend."

Lesley bristled at his intuition. "As a matter of fact, we did have a falling-out."

"Over what? Your cooking?"

Lesley gritted her teeth and smiled. "Not exactly. Over the right to make my own decisions."

"Such as?"

"Such as whether or not to take this job." The same anger that had driven her to sever the relationship returned, suffusing her with irritation and propelling her to her feet. "It was his warped opinion that journalism is man's work, that I didn't have a chance of competing with the big male fish." Her jaw tightened as her gaze fixed on the enveloping shield of trees. "He told me that I was better suited writing for a *society* column, covering wedding dresses and birth announcements." She turned and glared at Richard. *"Babies,"* she said hotly. "I wanted to get out there and make something of myself, and he wanted me to write columns about babies!"

Richard ran his finger along the rough armrest of his chair. "Were you two engaged?"

"Not even close."

"Living together?"

She shook her head. "No. That's not my style."

Richard nodded in acknowledgment, then shrugged. "If I had to guess, I'd probably say that journalism is a tough profession, too. Did you ever think that maybe he knew what was best for you?"

Keep it together, Lesley told herself, when his words threatened to push her over the edge. "Never once," she said with conviction.

Richard watched Wolf chase a squirrel up a birch tree. "You shouldn't be so quick to say that. You should be more open to other people's opinions. You're a lot like Dad. He won't listen to reason, either."

"'Reason'?" Lesley echoed in a low voice. "You call degrading someone's chosen profession and trying to rule their life, reason?"

"I've never berated Dad's ability to run a boarding house, and I certainly don't rule his life," he answered, rubbing a booted foot over a loose plank on the veranda. "I just happen to know what's best for him. He'll come around. Eventually."

A lump of indignation stuck in Lesley's throat. Just as well, she thought, gazing out over to where Wolf was now digging in the dirt. It might help her keep her thoughts on meddling busybodies to herself and keep her from blowing her cover.

"Well, it's real sweet of you to think for all of us who can't do it for ourselves," she said, turning back to him with an intense stare. "But I'm doing just fine on my own, and I think your father is, too."

He shrugged. "Matter of opinion." Wolf returned to the veranda, wagging his tail sharply. "Listen," Richard said, rising. "I have to feed this guy now, or he'll start chewing on my ankle. Did you want to see the inside of the cabin yet?"

Lesley hesitated, surprised by Richard's sudden change of topic. He obviously hadn't been as affected by their conversation as she had. He hadn't been out to prove anything by telling her that he knew what was best for his father, he was simply stating what he believed to be fact. His acceptance that she knew better took the wind out of her sails and left her struggling for words.

"Oh, uh, y-yes. I'd love to see the inside," she stammered, hating his ability to throw her off balance.

He smiled easily and ushered her inside. "This is it," he said, following closely. "Home sweet home. Take a look around. Anything you want to know about me, you'll find out here."

A quick retort came to Lesley's mind but she bit it back. She was, after all, supposed to be playing the simpering female.

Stepping over the curled edge of the heavy rug, she looked around the room, from the battered brown plaid sofa covered with a gaudy print blanket, half on, half off, to the tiny kitchen facilities, to the ivory upright piano in the corner. The solid log walls were covered with old maps, discolored photographs in antique frames, horseshoes, rusty tools and every other conceivable knickknack. The floor of pine strips was grooved through years of wear, and covered in spots with dusty, hand-hooked rugs.

"It's fascinating," Lesley whispered.

"Ergo, I'm fascinating?"

She turned and scanned his face, her eyes seeing a completely different side to the man she thought she'd figured out days ago. Which one was the real Richard Conway? The bossy extrovert who forced his opinions on others, or the proud inhabitant of a tiny cabin nestled in the backwoods of Alaska?

"Oh, you're fascinating, all right," she answered carefully.

He tilted his head in acknowledgment. "Thanks. Hold that thought. We'll get back to it in a minute." He waved around the room. "But first, the five-dollar tour. Now, this was the first house Mum and Dad lived in when they came to Alaska as newlyweds," he explained. "Most of the photographs are hers. Only a few are mine. Things I've picked up along the way usually end up on the wall, too. Or in the bookcases." He motioned to one of three stacked to the hilt with books, papers and ornaments. "Keeps them out of the way." He turned to her. "Care for some coffee?"

"Hmm? Oh, no thanks," she said absently, catching sight of the hot plate and minuscule fridge. "What's through there?" she asked, motioning with her hand.

"The bedroom." He pushed the door open to reveal a smaller room dominated by a king-size bed covered in a thick eiderdown quilt and several over-size pillows.

Better stay out of that room.

"Very nice," she admitted, surveying the bedroom from the doorway. She returned to the living room, immediately crossing to the old wooden piano. "Do you play?" she asked, lifting the cover and running her fingers along the yellowed keys.

"'Fraid not," he said, filling Wolf's dish with dry dog food. "My mother tried to teach me, but I was a lost cause. Couldn't imagine learning it when all you had to do was ask her to play." He came over to Lesley and lifted a framed picture from the high top of the piano. "This was her at twenty, just married and on her way to live in Alaska."

"So she wasn't a native-born Alaskan?"

Richard shook his head. "Nope. Born and bred in Maine, of all places. Talk about culture shock." He chuckled. "Still, she came here with an open mind and learned to love it."

Lesley carefully put the picture back and took a seat on what looked to be a hand-carved wooden rocking chair while Richard pushed a pile of technical maga-zines aside and sat down on the rough log coffee table by her feet. Propping his elbows on his knees, he leaned forward and smiled back at her.

"So do you like what you see?"

A warm breeze blew in through the large open win-dow in the corner, ruffling the simple curtains and sending Richard's scent across to Lesley. It was fresh, masculine and musky, and she had to fight the urge to forgive and forget the fact that he was, at that mo-ment, trying to sweet-talk her into leaving his father's home.

"I think your cabin is very attractive," she began slowly. "The same way I think *you're* extremely attractive."

"You do?"

"Of course I do. You're tall, and masculine, with gorgeous brown hair." She ran a hand through it to prove her point. "But there's something else," she added, swallowing hard as she contemplated how to tell him that she knew what he was up to.

It was a moot point, for at that moment, Richard slid a hand around the back of her neck and pulled her forward. His scent immediately surrounded her. His presence overwhelmed her. Against her better judgment, she melted into his embrace and welcomed his lips upon hers. A gentle caress of his tongue and her lips parted, forcing a groan of desire from deep within her.

I'm losing my sanity, she thought hazily, and I don't care. The realization sent a jolt through her, and she laid her hands on Richard's chest and pushed away.

"Uh, I—I don't usually work this fast," she stammered.

"Neither do I," he assured her, "but there's something about you, Lesley…I'm not sure what it is. I'm not sure I want to know. At this point—" he dragged his lips along her neck leaving behind a trail of hot kisses "—I'd rather we just both enjoy it."

Lesley felt her stomach tighten.

"You feel it, too, don't you?" Richard asked, snapping Lesley's thoughts back. He threaded his fingers through her hair and framed her face with his hands so she had no choice but to meet his gaze. "Tell the truth, Lesley."

She couldn't. She wouldn't. There was nothing to tell. She would not allow herself to be gulled by this man who had, by his own admission, every intention of somehow forcing her to leave Alaska.

This is just another ploy, Lesley. Don't be—

"Tell me, Lesley." His voice was strong, demanding.

A heady, excited tingle coursed through her. Heaven help me, she thought frantically, but I'm going to admit the truth, the whole truth and nothing but the truth.

"Yes," she whispered. "Yes, I do feel it." His lips met hers again in a gentle but firm kiss that forced her head back. He cupped her neck with his warm hand to steady her while she laid her hand on his chest and felt his heartbeat.

She pulled away first, her breathing stilted and ragged.

"Why don't we go somewhere more comfortable?" Richard suggested, nodding toward the bedroom.

Lesley hesitated, wishing for one sweet moment that she could take Richard up on his offer. She reached out and drew a shaky hand along his unshaven cheek, smiling wistfully as its roughness assaulted her soft palm. With barely restrained desire, she outlined his lips with her fingertip, catching her breath when his tongue came out to stop its journey with a gentle caress.

"I'd love to," she whispered, "but I can't."

"Tell me why, Lesley," he ordered quietly.

She took a deep breath and drew her hand away.

"Because I know what you're up to."

Chapter Four

Richard stilled. "You know what I'm up to?"

"Mmm-hmm," Lesley told him sweetly. Her heart was hammering in her breast, but she forced herself to appear calm. "I know all about your little plan to talk me into leaving Conway House." She straightened his collar and smoothed it down with her palm, reluctant to lose physical contact. "A few kisses, some kind words and poof! I'm out of your father's life. Unfortunately, that's just not going to happen."

He hesitated, then jumped up. "What!" He jammed his hands on his hips. "You think that's what this is all about?"

Lesley straightened her sweater. "No, I *know* that's what it's all about." She stood up and smoothed her hair behind her ears. "Lord knows, I've eaten enough of my mother's turnip and liver to know what you're up to."

Turnip? Liver? Where had that come from? "Well, you're *wrong*."

"No, I'm not. And your getting angry proves it. Your little scheme backfired, and now you're throwing a tantrum. Bucky, I've got an older brother. I've seen him in action. This sweet-talking stuff is something I know about."

"The hell you do," he snapped, running a hand along the back of his neck. That Lesley had figured out what he'd been trying to do was bad enough, that she was gloating was unforgivable. "And don't compare me to someone else."

"Why not?" she said with a laugh. "You're just like him. If he couldn't bully me into doing something, then he'd bribe me with candy. Then, when ju-jubes didn't work anymore, he went back to bullying. God!" she said, running her fingers through the loose hair at her temple and staring into space. "I can't believe my lousy luck. No matter where I go, I get stuck with these, these..."

"These what?" Richard demanded with a frown. Damn, she was talking crazy. "These what?"

She shot him a fierce, penetrating glare. "Men who need to control me."

"Control you?" he asked in disbelief. "You're joking, right?"

"No, I'm not," she shot back. She took a step forward, shortening the gap between them. "You brought me here today to use mind control to get me out of your life."

He stared at her. "Jeez, I'd heard about people like you, but I never figured I'd meet one."

"Like what?" she snarled.

"Like whacko, Toots. Like so way out in left field, you couldn't catch the ball if it landed in your mitt."

"Why don't you speak English?"

"Why don't you wake up and smell the coffee? *Mind* control?"

She huffed and straightened, then folded her arms in a defiant knot. "Tell me I'm wrong. Tell me you had no intention of talking me into leaving Conway House when you brought me here today."

Richard shifted from one foot to another. "Okay," he conceded. "Maybe at first—"

"Here it comes," she muttered.

"Maybe at first, I thought I might…talk some sense into you."

"Talk sense," she said, shaking her head.

Richard forced his irritation back. "But after I got you here, I realized that I was honestly attracted to you."

"Ha!" Lesley unfolded her arms and propped them on her hips, mimicking Richard's stance.

He immediately folded his arms across his chest.

"Do I *look* like I just fell off the turnip truck, Mr. Conway?"

She was doing it again, he thought darkly. Getting him so worked up he couldn't think straight. He took a minute to calm down, then spoke in his best business tone of voice.

"I admit that at first I thought I might be able to convince you to leave," he began piously. "But then, when I got you here and we started talking, I realized that…" He took a deep breath, a sudden and blinding discovery hitting him broadside. He was speaking the truth. Looking her in the eye, he smiled and lowered his voice. "I'm attracted to you."

"Uh-huh."

His smile faded at the disbelieving look on her face. Her expression insinuated that he was still playing games.

"And I suppose," she said slowly, "that if I was willing to leave Conway House—now, today—you'd try to stop me?"

"Well, no."

"See!"

She crossed her arms and Richard jammed his fists back on his hips.

"So what's your next plan of attack?" she asked, with a provoking laugh. "Are you going to put snakes in my bed? Or maybe set Marty, your pet squirrel, on me?"

"Actually I had something else in mind."

"As long as it doesn't include you and me being within ten feet of each other," she said, still laughing, "I'll survive."

Richard watched her head for the front door, his frown fading into a slow grin. She didn't know it yet, but she'd just given him Plan C, in which one Richard Buck Conway stuck like glue to one Lesley Toots Lyndstrom, driving her so crazy with his presence that she would be begging to leave Conway House. He ran through the logistics and decided it would work. And even if it didn't, he'd get to spend time around a woman who—for reasons unknown—he was honestly attracted to.

"Why are you smiling like that?" Lesley asked, watching him through narrowed eyes.

"No reason," he answered smoothly. He came up beside her and opened the door. "Ready to go?"

She drew her arm from his light grasp and made her way to the truck. "Sure," she said warily. "But what are you up to?"

"Who, me?" He feigned innocence. "Why, Lesley. What makes you think I'm up to anything?"

"Woman's intuition." She allowed him to settle her in the passenger seat of the truck. "And the fact that you're a man."

Richard shut the door behind her and skimmed around the front hood. She glared at him through the windshield, but he simply smiled back and whistled to Wolf who came bounding out of the bush and jumped into the cab of the truck beside Lesley.

The woman was fooling herself if she believed for a minute that she could outsmart him, he thought, shoving the keys into the ignition and revving the truck's engine.

The sight of her crammed against the truck door vainly trying to avoid Wolf's sloppy kisses made him laugh out loud.

Maybe Wolf could help him with Plan C. She didn't seem to like the animal any more than she liked its owner. Maybe if the two of them stayed by her side for a while, they'd get the job done quicker.

It was worth a try, and besides, what did he have to lose?

Lesley drew a heavy black line through the typewritten words on her page, groaned and tossed her pencil onto the high pile of articles, magazines and photographs atop her desk. In less than a week, her desk had come to look just like her boss's, with the exception of the ten Twinkies snack-cake wrappers that usually littered Mae's.

The office was empty and quiet save the occasional telephone call and the gentle hum of the traffic below the open window. John, the photographer, a pleasant young man in his late twenties, was not scheduled to come in again for several days, and the receptionist was away on an extended weekend. The double issue of *Northern Man Monthly* to be released in a month's time was going well and would be finished on schedule. The only regret that Lesley had concerning her job, in fact, was that she hadn't gotten it sooner.

Everything was running like clockwork, so why, she wondered, was she feeling so out of sorts? She huffed thoughtfully and picked up a glossy photograph of a handsome older man with attractive blond features. She stared at his face with disinterest. She'd interviewed him just last Friday, and he'd been polite, attentive and...bland. Not nearly as charismatic as Richard. If you liked charisma.

Lesley heard Mae's familiar heavy shuffle and looked up as the woman approached her desk.

"What's the matter, hon?" Mae asked brightly. She raised her eyebrows and propped her girth on the corner of Lesley's desk. "Does the man defy description?"

Her good humor made Lesley laugh. No matter how overwhelming her first week at work had been, no matter how tired she was from doing both the cooking and cleaning at the boardinghouse, no matter how concerned her mood when she remembered Richard's smug smile after the fiasco at his cabin, Mae could always make her laugh.

Lesley scanned the photograph again, then dropped it onto the pile of others. "First thing Monday morn-

ing, I guess everyone defies description." She laughed
lightly. "So how was your weekend, boss lady?"

She shrugged. "Nothing to write home about." A
shrewd look in Lesley's direction. "So how's every
little thing at Conway House?" Her tone was casual
enough, but Lesley knew that behind that lovable fa-
cade lay a shrewd and intuitive mind. One always had
to choose their words carefully when around Mae
Barker.

"It's busy. The first guests arrived last Thursday
and I've been going ever since." She leaned back in her
padded office chair and stretched her arms above her
head. "It's a lot of work, especially the cooking, but
it sure is interesting, meeting all these new people. A
lot are lifelong friends of Bob's so it's not really like
being in charge of a hotel, or anything like that."

"Whatever happened to the idea of hiring a cook?"

"It died when the last housekeeper left and gave
Conway House such a bad name that no one in the
state of Alaska wants to work there," Lesley teased.

"That must be Buck's doing."

Lesley's eyes darted to Mae's. So she knew.

"I'm afraid so." She blew a heavy breath through
her lips. "Not that I've seen him this past week. He
disappeared right after..."

"Mmm-hmm," Mae said, clicking her teeth. "Got
it."

Lesley flushed and fiddled with her pencil. "It's
nothing like that, Mae. It's just, oh..." She made the
mistake of looking into Mae's interested eyes and the
next thing she knew, she was telling the woman all
about Richard's unsuccessful attempts to get her to
leave the boardinghouse.

"Why, that little bossy-butt," Mae said with a wry smile. "He's just as bad as I thought he was." She chuckled as though his irritating nature appealed to her, then smiled down at Lesley. "What you need to do, hon, is teach our Bucky a lesson."

I already tried that, Lesley thought grimly.

"And I'm *just* the person to help you," Mae added brightly.

"You?"

"Well, of course, honey." She held her hands palm up and cocked an eyebrow. "Who better?"

Lesley watched Mae's smile broaden, if that were possible. Who better indeed, she thought, wondering exactly what her boss had in mind. Sometimes Mae came out with such wild ideas, it was hard to believe that she'd gotten anywhere in life. Her enthusiasm was only slightly less vibrant than her clothes, and today she looked as if she'd dressed in the dark, with her garishly bright dress and mismatched bauble earrings that accentuated the darkness of her hair.

"Okay," Lesley said with a disbelieving grin. "I'll bite. How can you help me out?"

"*I'll* move into Conway House."

"What?"

"Sure! I'd love to!" Mae jumped from the table, taking half the papers with her. "*I* happen to love to cook, but I've got no one but Ping and Pong to do it for," she said, referring to her two beloved Siamese cats. "And you hate to cook, right?"

"Right," Lesley answered warily.

"Well, then? Doesn't it only make sense that I move in and help you out?"

Lesley considered it. "Well, uh...no, not really. I mean, you have a house, a life and a job here at the magazine. Why would you—"

"Because I love people, hon. Or haven't you noticed?"

Oh, I've noticed, Lesley thought wryly. There was no more gregarious woman alive than their Mae Barker. Outgoing and sociable, Mae had a knack for making friends by the bucketful. But it wasn't enough. She needed more. More people and more activity. Come to think about it, maybe the boardinghouse was the perfect place for her. It was busy, noisy and Lord knew, Lesley could use help with the cooking.

"Besides," Mae continued. "I've been wanting to get my house painted for a while. This would be the perfect opportunity to have it done, inside and out, without getting in the painters' way."

There was an awkward hesitation. "I'm not sure I have the right to offer you a place at Conway House, though."

"Well, ask Bob, then. I've met him once or twice. He seems like a reasonable man. And he loves to irritate Buck." She smiled at Lesley's revealing look. "You bet I know. Everyone loves to irritate Buck. He's a blowhard know-it-all. He asks for it." She winked conspiratorially. "What's say we give him a run for his George Washingtons? Go on. Call Bob. See what he says."

Mae winked again, grabbed a cup of coffee and Danish pastry from the side counter and left, toasting Lesley with the sugary dessert as she passed her desk.

Lesley considered Mae's words long after the woman had returned to her office and begun to pore over the newest batch of paperwork on her desk.

Maybe she had a point. It was slow at the office right now, and Conway House did need help. More guests were due to arrive the following day, and much as she loved the work, Lesley was having trouble with the culinary aspect of her obligation. Maybe Mae's moving in would work, at that.

A little devil appeared on Lesley's shoulder. Yes, he whispered in her ear, but it would send Richard through the roof. He would be furious. He'd yell the house down. He wouldn't be able to sleep nights knowing that his objective of closing Conway House had moved that much farther out of reach.

A sinful smile crossed Lesley's lips, and she picked up the phone.

Richard winced at the hot water coming from the mudroom tap.

"What do you *mean*, move in?" he demanded of Lesley, who was leaning against the doorframe. She looked cool as a cucumber, poised and smug, undoubtedly pleased that she'd been the one to drop this latest bomb on him.

He'd spent the week since their confrontation at the cabin flying groups of fishermen around the state for a buddy who operated a tour group. The time away had given him an opportunity to recall in embarrassing detail how Lesley had seen through his plan to sweet-talk her out of his father's house. Damn, she was good. But he was better—and he had spent the past seven days honing his plan to stick by Lesley's side and drive her away with his personality. Not very flattering, but hey, this was war. And now there was Mae....

"Tell me you're not serious," he demanded, grabbing a towel and scrubbing his hands dry. "Tell me you haven't invited that modern-day Medusa to stay at the house."

Lesley smiled but said nothing. Her supremely challenging stance—arms crossed over her chest and one leg bent as she leaned against the doorframe—did not go unnoticed by Richard. Actually, nothing had gone unnoticed from the moment she'd shown up ten minutes ago. Because of the heat, she was dressed in a loose pair of baggy pants and matching top in the same shade of blue as her eyes. The same eyes he'd gazed into a week ago that had made him think he'd glimpsed nirvana. Had he known that he was staring into the eyes of a she-devil who would haunt his days and nights, he'd have run the other way, and fast.

"Well, tell her it's a no-go," he said, throwing a towel into a laundry bin with more force than necessary. He turned to Lesley and rubbed the back of his neck. "Tell her the deal's off. Dad'll never go for it, anyway."

"As a matter of fact, he was thrilled when I told him she could move in today."

"You've already *told* him?"

"Mmm-hmm." She took a step forward and laid a hand on his chest. Like her touch, her scent was light and feminine, and it was all Richard could do not to grab her by the shoulders and kiss her senseless. "It's all arranged," she whispered. "In fact, she's already moved her stuff in." She traced a line on the fabric of his plaid shirt, and he felt his gut tighten. And when her face tilted toward him, his desire skyrocketed. "Face it, Bucky. You've been outsmarted."

She tapped his chest lightly, then with a little laugh stepped back.

"Guess again, Toots," Richard ground out, grabbing her as he'd envisioned, and dragging her forward while he took her lips in a crushing kiss. She resisted, then quickly relaxed within his arms. He felt her arms slide around his waist and suddenly drew back himself. She was intoxicating, wicked and he wanted her. The knowledge bugged him to no end.

He jerked her away from his responsive body, his hands still on her shoulders. She looked indignant and wiped her lips with the back of her hand.

"Don't do that again," she warned with a scathing glare.

"Don't provoke me again," he shot back. He lowered his hands and pointed a finger at her. "Because that's what you'll get every time you do."

"Not likely."

"Count on it."

"Guess again."

"Good morning, boys and girls! And how are my two most favorite people in the whole wide world today?"

Richard groaned loudly. Today was not a good day for Mae Barker and her unflagging exuberance. He looked past Lesley's shoulder and saw the woman gently lower two cats to the floor.

"What the hell— Who are *they?*" he demanded.

"Ping and Pong," Mae said with a smile. "They're my babies. Wherever I go, they go."

Richard sent her an exaggerated smile. "Then why don't you fire up that broom of yours and take them back to *your* house?"

Mae threw her head back and laughed out loud. "Good one, Bucky. I think I'm gonna have a good time here. *Real* good," she added with a wink to a chuckling Lesley.

"Would you like me to show you around the kitchen?" Lesley offered.

"No, thanks," Mae said with a wave of her hand. "I'll find everything I need. Don't worry about me. I'm going to take inventory, then go for groceries. Bob's told me how many guests are coming, so I know what I need." She smiled brightly. "Why don't you kids go off somewhere and have a little fun? It's a nice day, and you're not due into the office, Les."

"Count me out," Richard said sharply, sliding past Lesley. "This place is too crazy for me. I'm going for a ride."

Lesley's ears perked up. She'd been hoping for an opportunity like this to arise. She still hadn't figured out Richard's newest plan to get rid of her, although she was sure he had one. Granted, he was a formidable adversary, but even the best slipped up. What she needed to do was to spend as much time as possible with him. Watch and listen to what he did and said until she knew him better than he knew himself. It was perfect, and besides, what did she have to lose?

Lesley ignored the voice in her head that accused her of looking for a way to spend time with Richard and said, "I'd love to go for a ride." She followed him through the mudroom and out the back door. "I've never been on a horse before. It would be good research, don't you think?"

He stopped so quickly that she bumped into him from behind. Her hands immediately came up to brace herself on his back, an entirely pleasant sensation since he was wearing a thinner shirt and no jacket today. Lesley felt the heat of his skin through the fabric and fought the urge to run her hands along his spine.

He turned to her and she reluctantly lost physical contact. "You're joking, right?" he said, looking at her in amazement. "You've never been on a horse?"

"Nope," she said, almost proudly. "Would you like to teach me the ropes?"

"Do I have a choice?"

She gave him a winning smile. "Nope."

He stared at her for several seconds, then shrugged. "Maybe it's just as well. El Diablo hasn't been out in a week. He could use a good run."

Lesley's step slowed as she trailed behind Richard. "El Diablo?" Didn't that mean "devil" in some foreign language? Surely Richard was pulling her leg? They entered the barn where he saddled up the biggest, blackest horse she'd ever seen and then handed her the reins. She hazarded a look into the horse's bright eyes and felt her legs begin to shake. "Don't you have any ponies I could practice on?"

Richard led the mare—the one who had greeted them the day they'd had their argument—from a stall and coaxed a metal bit into her velvety mouth.

"Sorry, no ponies."

The massive black horse by her side snorted loudly and stamped the ground. "Are you going to ride that one?" she asked, nodding toward the mare.

"Yep," Richard answered in a cowboy twang. "Cream Puff 'n me go back a long way."

"Cream Puff?" El Diablo snorted and again tossed his head. "Couldn't we switch, or something?" Lesley asked, stiff as a board, but trying to sound brave. Her arms and legs felt weak and she knew the demon horse from hell by her side was sizing her up, probably laughing, in its own horsey way.

Richard led both horses outside and sighed thoughtfully. "I don't know." He looked out over the deserted yard, then back to her. "What's it worth?"

"Anything," she promised. *"Anytime."*

He gave another thoughtful sigh, rubbed the back of his neck and stared at her for several long seconds. "Well . . . okay. But you owe me one."

"I won't forget," she assured him, then watched Richard cup his hands together to help her up onto Cream Puff. "What are you doing? You haven't put the saddle on yet."

"I know. I don't use one. Up you go."

"But, but—" Lesley's words ended in a screech when she found herself on the back of the horse. Her back was as stiff as a two-by-four, her knuckles white and unbending as they held the reins. She looked at the hard-packed ground, then just as quickly squeezed her eyes shut. "I can't do this. Get me down."

"Relax and take it easy," Richard told her. "Horses can sense fear."

Lesley's screams for mercy caught in her throat. *So this is how it's going to end. I'm going to be escorted to the pearly gates on horseback.*

"I can't take it easy," she croaked. "I'm about to die."

"Not true." Richard swung up into the saddle of El Diablo and reined him in. "Cream Puff wouldn't hurt a fly." He urged his horse down the back path that led away from the barn and into the shrub, clicking his teeth so the mare would follow suit. "Just don't let her take you underneath any low bushes. She likes to get rid of riders that way."

Lesley choked back a tortured shriek. Other than staying beside her, Richard didn't seem all that concerned about her safety.

"I'll never forgive you for this, Buck Conway. I swear on all that I hold dear, one day I'll get you for this."

Richard laughed off her threats and took a deep, contented breath. "Isn't this great?" he said enthusiastically. "Just you, and me and the horses—oh."

"Oh what?"

"Oh, nothing. It's just…has anyone told you about Alaskan coral snakes yet?"

"Alaskan…snakes!" She hadn't read about snakes in Alaska, but then maybe she'd skimmed over that part in her travel guide.

"Yeah, real mean critters." Richard hissed lowly. "Maybe you'd better not get off Cream Puff until I debrief you."

"But what if I *fall* off?"

He shot her a sympathetic smile. "These things happen."

Lesley had had enough. She wanted to accuse Richard of lying, of trying to frighten her, but she couldn't be sure that what he was saying was a joke. She looked out the corner of her eye at the underbrush that ran along the edge of the trail. There sure was a lot of it. Rocks, broken trees and fallen logs, too. The best snake breeding ground in the country from the look of it.

"I don't believe you," she said bravely.

"About the snakes?"

Another covert glance downward. "About anything. I think you're trying to scare me into leaving since your other plans didn't work."

He looked over and smiled. "Trying to figure me out again, Toots?" He laughed. "Don't bother. First, I'm too complicated, and second, I'm not up to anything."

Lesley could have sworn she heard him mutter "much" under his breath. There just was no saying with this guy.

"Just remember I'm on to you, and I don't believe a word you say. Especially about the snakes."

"So get off your horse."

"No!" Damn, she had fallen for his teasing again. His deep, throaty laughter echoed through the trees, filling the moment, and her heart, with unexpected warmth. She should be angry with him for all the frustration he caused her, but somehow that anger wouldn't come.

"So, Madam Fortune-teller. Tell me. What am I up to?"

She considered it. "I think you're trying to scare me into leaving Alaska with fake stories of these coral snakes of yours."

"You don't see me getting off my horse, do you?"

Lesley stifled an irritated growl. "Admit it, Bucky. You're up to something. Men like you are always up to something."

"Men like me?"

"Don't play dumb." They continued down the path, her horse's heavy, plodding step and swaying gait an increasingly soothing balm to her churning insides. "You're using your personality to control me, and your physical size to overwhelm me."

"Jeez, Toots. You make me sound like a sex-starved Viking about to pillage you on horseback. Not very flattering, and not very accurate, either."

"How *would* you describe yourself, then?"

He took a deep breath and reined El Diablo to a halt. He turned to Lesley, his arm braced on his leg and his face creased in a thoughtful frown.

"I'd say I'm a pretty honest, straightforward sort of guy. One who cares about the world and people around him. A man who is sensitive and understanding...with the greatest set of buns—"

"Oh, never mind!" Lesley sighed, urging Cream Puff on. "I should have known I wouldn't get a straight answer from you."

Richard followed close behind. "Careful. I think Cream Puff's up to something."

Lesley felt the horse veer to the right and yanked on the reins. She knew immediately that it was overcompensation, and seconds later she found herself sliding off the horse's smooth back like butter from a hot knife. She called out in surprise, but it did nothing to stop her descent. She landed in an ungraceful pile on the hard ground.

Richard was beside her in seconds, pulling her to her feet.

"See what you made me do?" she said through frustrated tears. She was trying so hard to keep her cool, yet failing miserably.

"What *I* made you do? Toots, I hate to break this to you, but you fell off on your own."

"You scared me," she insisted, allowing his hands to remain on her shoulders. They felt heavy and warm and protective. "You always seem to scare me."

He brushed the hair from her face. "I don't mean to."

She looked into his eyes. He certainly seemed sincere. No smile hovered about his lips, no laughter tinged his tone.

"You weren't in danger," he added, running a finger along her cheek. "I was right here. I'd never let anything happen to you."

She couldn't seem to pull her gaze away from his. "Maybe not intentionally."

"Not ever," he insisted gently.

His gaze was too intense for her. Too ripe with innuendo and unspoken questions. Damn him, but she didn't have the answers. To fracture the invisible hold, she pulled from his embrace and roughly brushed at the seat of her pants.

"I don't like falling," she said crisply.

"No one does." He shortened the gap between them. "But these things happen in life. We can't always help it."

Lesley swallowed hard and looked up into his eyes. "I can," she said firmly.

"Then you are a very special lady, Miss Lyndstrom." He reached out and smoothed her hair back. "Much stronger than I am, in fact."

She laughed nervously when his hand lingered. "Don't be silly. You're one of the strongest men I've ever met."

He hesitated, then lowered his hand. Lesley regretted the loss of contact, then chastised herself for being contrary, reminding herself that she didn't like it when he took liberties. It made her feel giddy and irresponsible.

"I used to think I was fearless," he murmured. "But now I'm not so sure."

He reached for her mount, turning the horse slightly so she could get back on. She did so, with trepidation, then looked down to where he stood by her thigh.

"But what could a man like you be afraid of?"

He gave a hollow laugh and met her gaze. "Funny enough, falling. I guess I'm just like you. Afraid of falling."

He handed her the reins, which she took in shaky fingers, and he swung up onto El Diablo, looking for all the world like the self-sufficient survivor she knew him to be.

"Try not to fall again," he said casually. A nudge to his horse's middle and they set off. "For both our sakes." He gave Lesley a penetrating look that made her sit up a bit straighter. "Because if you do, I might do something stupid and be right behind you."

Chapter Five

Lesley looked from the depths of her teacup into the eyes of one of the more cordial male guests. Tall and slight with a crop of reddish brown hair, he was an attractive man who had taken an instant liking to Lesley on his arrival at Conway House three days earlier.

"Hmm? I'm sorry, I didn't catch that," she admitted, trying to focus on his words.

"I was saying that you really should see the Spirit Houses in Eklutna. Apparently the Indians use them instead of headstones. A small one means a child's grave, a tiny house inside a large house means a mother and child were buried together—that sort of thing." He slid an arm along the sofa, close to Lesley's shoulders. "All very interesting, don't you think? How about we take a drive out to see them before I leave?"

Lesley smiled and nodded vaguely. "Sure. Why not?"

Her words were directed to the man beside her, but her eyes were watching the tall dark figure who sat across the noisy lounge, alone, drinking beer from a glass as he flipped through a wildlife magazine. The beer's foam coated his upper lip, and Lesley found herself licking her own lip in response. Richard's mouth fascinated her. She'd only come in contact with it a few times, but each time it had extracted from her a heady response that made her ache to taste more.

She shifted in her seat, immediately regretting the movement. Her backside and legs were still sore from the ride she'd taken with Richard yesterday and would probably stay that way for several days as a living reminder of their time together.

How very appropriate, she thought smartly, that a pain in her rear end should remind her of Richard. Besides teasing her about the horses—whose real names were Caesar and Lizzy—there was his phony snake story. Alaskan coral snakes indeed! She'd never forget how Mae and Bob and the half-dozen guests at the dinner table had roared with laughter when she'd shared Richard's little lecture with them. When she'd learned that there were no known species of snakes in Alaska, she could have choked Richard. And if her arms hadn't hurt too much to raise them, that's exactly what she would have done. Maybe she still would.

"…And then maybe we could take in the tidal bore along Turnagain Arm. I hear the waves can reach ten feet high."

Lesley sipped her tea, nodded to the man by her side and realized she hadn't heard a word he'd said…again. Turning toward him and forcing herself to concentrate, she nearly spilled her tea when Richard's voice broke into the guest's rhetoric.

"Speaking of crashing bores," he said smoothly, "mind if I interrupt?" He took Lesley's arm and lifted her from the sofa. "We'll be right back," he told the surprised guest.

Richard led Lesley over to the French doors and out onto the covered porch. It was as empty as the lounge was full, and he ushered her to a white wicker chair before sitting down himself.

"Why did you do that?" Lesley asked, realizing that she still had her teacup. She sipped the spice tea, but it was cool and unappealing. Her friend back in the lounge must have been talking longer than she realized. She put the cup down on the glass-top table and gingerly nestled into her seat.

"You needed rescuing." He looked out over the grassy field of wildflowers. "The guy you were talking to was hitting you up for a roll in the hay, in case you hadn't noticed."

Lesley's jaw dropped. "He was not! Besides, what's it to you who I spend my nights with?"

"Nothing. It's nothing to me. I just don't want any bad publicity coming out of Conway House. Your being dragged off into the backwoods and assaulted might give us a bad name."

Lesley couldn't believe what she was hearing. "Gosh, thanks *so* much for your concern, but for your information, Mr. Conway, I am not some bleached blond bubblehead who doesn't know her knee from her elbow where men are concerned. I know all about—"

"Men and sexual attraction? Jeez, that's a relief."

Lesley bit the inside of her lip. "Is there anything else you'd like to say before I return to our guests?"

"Yeah," he said, sitting forward in his seat. His gaze was dark and penetrating, and pushed her back in her chair. "Don't be gulled by *any* of the guys around here. They might be looking for more than you're willing to give."

Lesley had had enough. She, too, leaned forward in her wicker chair and gave Richard a wide-eyed look of concern.

"Gosh, Bucky. Does that include you? Are you looking for more than I'm willing to give?"

She gave a little laugh and sat back, closing her eyes and enjoying the fragrant woodsy smell of early evening. Pine trees, fresh air, flowers ... Richard.

Her eyes flew open. Richard was leaning over her chair, one hand on each armrest. The evening breeze had been the one to bring his scent to her. Soap. Leather. Heat.

"Why don't you tell me how much you're willing to give, and I'll tell you if it's enough?" he asked in a low voice.

Lesley tried to swallow the lump in her throat. It stuck, halfway down, and kept her silent. Her gaze drifted to the open collar of his shirt, to the warm pulse at the base of his throat, and the hint of dark hair that showed beneath the button band. Her hand moved toward the fabric before she pulled it back sharply.

"I'm not willing to give you anything," she whispered.

"Why not?" He ran a hand through the hair at her temple. "Aren't you attracted to me?"

"You're a very attractive man," she hedged.

"Glad you think so." His fingers teased her earlobe. "Then why aren't you willing to give me anything?"

"What do you want?"

His finger trailed down her neck to the open collar of her denim shirtwaist dress. "What if I said I want it all?" he asked, loosening the next button.

Lesley's spine shivered. She seemed to be moving in slow motion, if at all, while her brain seemed to have stopped working altogether. She swallowed, hard, her gaze glued to Richard's.

"Richard," she said, trying to maintain control. "You have to stop this game. What will the guests think if they see us?'

"But they can't see us. The plant, remember?"

Lesley should have remembered the bushy umbrella tree that blocked the view from the doors to the porch. She'd moved it there herself late yesterday.

Richard's finger disappeared beneath the denim and teased the lace of her camisole. His breathing was even and controlled, whereas hers was stilted and labored. His hand appeared as steady as a rock, whereas she seemed to be shaking from the inside out.

His finger gently caressed the heated skin beneath the silky undergarment, sending extra waves of warmth along Lesley's spine. Her eyes drifted closed. If she died right now, she'd die unsatisfied. She wanted more. She wanted Richard—lock, stock and barrel. A nagging voice reminded her of the pitfalls of falling for a man so totally unsuitable, but she ignored them. His touch extended farther and skimmed the peak of her breast, fueling her need to the breaking point.

He was intoxicating, and infuriating, and persuasive and overwhelming—

Lesley braced her shoulders and took a deep breath. Her hand came up to still his, pressing it close to her heart for a fraction of a second. He withdrew it of his own volition, and would have cupped her cheek had Lesley not gently grabbed his forearms and held him away.

"I can't do this," she said firmly.

"Why not?"

"It doesn't matter." He stood and she took the opportunity to cross to the edge of the porch and regain control of her spinning senses.

He followed, and leaned on the railing. "Why are you fighting me on this?" he asked calmly. "Even I can see that you'd like us to get closer." He traced a hand along her arm. "Why don't you let yourself go and be honest about what you're feeling?"

"I'm not feeling anything," she snapped, rubbing her arm. The memory of his touch remained, feeding her growing frustration. Her resolve was slipping away, abandoning her when she needed it the most. She felt limp and frighteningly vulnerable. "Don't look for emotions that aren't there."

"Liar," he whispered in her ear. His tongue drew her lobe between his lips. "You and I are going to come together one day, Lesley. Accept it."

She wouldn't, she thought angrily. She was stronger than that. Her feelings for Richard were fledgling. They could be denied and pushed back where they came from.

She took a step sideways and rubbed her ear as though it had been burnt. "Just how in hell do you know everything about everybody?" She fussed with her belt. "You don't know what I'm thinking. You don't know what I want. Hell!" she said raggedly. "*I* don't even know what I want."

Her sharp words echoed around the porch, inadvertently scaring away a gray jay who'd been feeding from a hanging bird feeder. She braced her hands on the rough wooden railing and lowered her head, denying the frustration that threatened her composure.

She had only a moment alone with her jumbled thoughts before Richard came up behind her and slid his arms around her waist. One gentle tug and Lesley was nestled back against his chest.

"You want me," he insisted, caressing her temple with a kiss, "as much as I want you." He pushed her hair aside with his cheek and trailed kisses down her neck. "Admit it, Lesley. Tell the truth."

Her head drifted back onto his shoulder. "I can't possibly want you. I don't even like your type of man."

He snuggled closer. "You don't have to like—" He hesitated. "What's wrong with men like me?"

"You're bossy," she answered honestly.

"No, I'm not."

The gray jay had returned to the feeder, settled, then flew off again at the sound of Richard's harsh denial.

"Yes, you are," Lesley insisted, feeling his withdrawal. "You're always telling people what to do with their lives. That's called being bossy and manipulative."

He pulled away completely, and Lesley shivered from the loss of contact.

"I'm *not* manipulative," he said, glowering at her. "Give me one example of when I've been manipulative," he demanded.

"When you tried to get rid of me the first time."

"Okay, two examples."

"When you tried to get rid of me the second time," she said, biting her lip to stifle a giggle.

Richard growled and ran a hand along the back of his neck. "You're way off, Toots. Just because I care about someone, doesn't mean I'm manipulative."

"You care about me?" she asked, with mock innocence.

"I didn't mean that. I meant that I cared enough about my father to try to get rid of you."

"Oh." She huffed and kept her gaze glued to the forest. "So you admit you were trying to run me out of town?"

"Sure. Wasn't that obvious?"

She turned to him. "Have you ever noticed how weird our conversations always get?"

He looked surprised. "That's not my fault. If you'd talk sense for once, that wouldn't happen."

"And what, to you, is sense?"

He smiled sensuously and stepped closer. "Knowing when you're attracted to someone and admitting it to that person."

"I told you, I'm not attracted to—"

Lesley's words were lost in a whoosh of air as she was dragged into Richard's embrace. Warm hands cupped her cheeks, holding her still as his mouth stole the words from her lips. She fought him briefly, just as quickly admitted defeat, then slid her own arms around his waist. His belt buckle dug into her softness, and still she pressed close until it became obvious that things were moving a little too quickly.

She was not surprised when Richard pulled back, but hadn't expected his smug grin.

"Not attracted, huh?" he said, cocking one eyebrow.

He dropped his hands and stood back, his gaze lingering on her tongue as it licked her gently swollen lips. She couldn't think of a thing to say. Her response had told all. To deny any attraction on her part would only make her look foolish.

He smiled at her silence and tapped the tip of her nose, then turned and headed for the doors to the lounge, his hands dug into his back jeans pocket. When he reached the door, he looked over his shoulder and gave Lesley a long, slow smile, the same one he'd given her the day they'd met at Mae's office.

Lesley tore her gaze away and tried to ignore his throaty laughter as it followed him into the lounge. She breathed deeply, three times, to combat the flush of her cheeks. If only he'd stay that infuriating, she thought tersely, she'd be safe from his charms. It was his gentle, caring side that knocked her off center and made her forget the promises she'd made herself before coming to Alaska.

The gray jay finished its meal and flew off in a noisy flurry of wings. In the distance, a tiny brown rabbit hopped along on its way somewhere, stopping every few feet before disappearing into the scrub. And from somewhere high in the aspen trees, she heard the vivid *chip, chip, chip,* of a tiny warbler.

Lesley felt her heartbeat return to normal and mentally ticked off her self-made promises. One, she was going to remain a journalist. Not a secretary, as her father wanted her to be, and not the stay-at-home society column writer that her ex-boyfriend had wanted her to become. Two, she was going to remain romantically unattached until she got her career in line and figured out exactly what kind of man she was looking for. And three, under no circumstances whatsoever was she going to fall for an overly confident, bossy man in the image of the male members of her family.

Well, at least I became a journalist. Northern Man Monthly was just a start, she knew, but at least it was a step in the right direction.

Lesley stayed outside for another ten minutes, relaxing to the sound of the friendly warbler's serenade. Then, when she felt she'd regained her composure, she picked up her teacup and returned to the lounge.

Several pairs of expectant eyes greeted her. Mae, who happened to be serving a large platter of after-dinner snacks, gave her a wink and a nudge as she passed. And the redheaded man she'd been talking to earlier was now deep in conversation with another guest. Lesley took a seat in a tub chair and grabbed two shrimp pastries from a platter on the coffee table. Richard must have said something on his way back through the lounge for her to be getting this sort of reception.

Lesley shoved the pastries in her mouth, biting down hard as she caught sight of Richard leaning against the doorway talking to a pretty local girl who'd come for dinner that evening.

Lesley grabbed two more pastries and stuffed them down, as well.

One of these days, Bucky, she thought, chewing furiously, *I'll get my chance to show you what I'm made of. And when I do, you'd better watch out.*

As it turned out, the opportunity arose four days later when Mae came bounding from her see-through office, her arms waving like an out-of-control windmill.

"Stop the presses!" she called loudly, although she and Lesley were the only people in the office. It was Lesley's turn to play reporter and receptionist that day, a job she liked since it brought her in contact with even more people than usual.

"Mae. Calm down, for heaven's sake," she said with a smile. "You're going to have a fit."

"I've already had a fit. Now I'm repeating my performance."

Lesley laughed and watched Mae throw a photograph on her desk. "That's him," she squawked. "That's the man who's done it to me."

Lesley recognized the young man instantly. He was their cover story.

"Do you know what our lover cover boy's gone and done?" Mae asked. "He's eloped! *Eloped!*" she repeated incredulously. "How could he do this to me?"

"I'm sure it's nothing personal, Mae," Lesley teased, picking up the photo. "Besides, I think it's romantic."

"Romantic! What the hell good is romantic to me? I'm running a magazine dating service here!" She tutted and shook her head. "Now who are we supposed to use?"

Lesley shrugged. "How about the one we choose as runner-up?"

"He's working on an oil rig in Northern Alberta. We agreed that he'd be the cover for the next issue, but I didn't see any point in getting the article done this far ahead. I've got no bio on him."

"Surely there's someone else we can use," Lesley said logically. "I mean, there are dozens of men dying to be in your magazine."

"True, but you know how long it takes to get an article done. The interview, the photographs, checking the guy out to make sure he's really single. We don't have that kind of time. The printer's already bugging me for the article so he can get the advance copies done."

Lesley sighed heavily. It did pose a problem. They'd worked hard to get this edition out on time. It would be a shame to be late just because of one silly glitch.

She leaned back in her chair and chewed on the end of her pencil. "What we need is someone we already know." She stared off into space. "Someone we know for sure is single. Someone good-looking...someone..."

A light went on in Lesley's brain and she turned her eyes to Mae, who sat perched on the edge of her desk, smiling deviously.

"You thinking what *I'm* thinking, honey?"

"I'm not sure," Lesley hedged. "What are you thinking?"

"I'm thinking our Bucky could just as easily be our cover boy this month, of course."

"He'd be furious," Lesley said with a gasp.

"You bet, hon. He'd hit the roof."

"He'd have our heads."

Mae gave one of her broad smiles that Lesley had long come to know meant trouble. "Yeah, but it'd be worth it to keep him out of your hair for a while."

Lesley nibbled her lower lip and tried to hold back her smile of approval. "Yeah, it'd be worth it," she growled finally.

A hearty whoop of laughter erupted from Mae. "Honey, I like your style! This is going to be good. *Real* good!"

That evening, Richard stretched his aching shoulders and flopped down on a sofa in the empty lounge. It had been a long day, the weather had made flying rough and, to top it off, the barn had needed to be cleaned out when he'd gotten home. Still, hard work never killed anyone, and one hot shower and he felt his old self again.

He leaned back on the pillow and flipped his feet up, remembering in detail the day he and Lesley had gone out riding and stopped by the small creek in the valley. After warning her not to drink any water that hadn't been boiled, he'd allowed her to paddle her feet in the refreshing stream as they talked of their respective childhoods.

He'd enjoyed listening to her stories. She was witty and bright, with a natural understanding of other people and their situations. She truly cared about others, and he could see now why the situation she'd been placed in with his father had been so upsetting.

As though drawn by his thoughts, Lesley walked into the room at that moment, a smile on her face and a high-tech camera around her neck.

"Hi," she said sweetly. "I thought I heard you come in."

"Hi, yourself." He swung his feet to the floor and braced his forearms on his thighs. "Taking up photography?" he asked, pointing to the camera.

"I'm trying to. John gave me a few pointers and let me borrow his camera, but..."

He watched her brow furrow slightly. "But?"

"Well, I've taken pictures of absolutely everything around here, but I want to practice on people now. Unfortunately, everyone's busy. Mae's cooking, your dad's out helping Old Man Marshall get his cows off the highway and, of course, I can't take a picture of myself.''

''Take one of me, then,'' he said, shrugging. ''If I'll do?''

''Oh, you'll do just fine,'' she gushed. ''Could we go outside, though? I'm not too good with the flash yet.''

''Sure.'' He followed her out onto the porch. ''How about here?'' he asked, leaning on the railing. She went down the steps and took several photos of him on the porch, a few of him sitting on the stairs and even one with his foot up on the tree stump. They then went to the corral. Then the barn. Then she wanted him to take his shirt off and make as though he was tossing hay with a pitchfork. Jeez, he thought an hour later, he'd created a monster.

''There, that's it,'' she said finally.

''Got what you wanted?''

''I think so. Now, I'll have to see if I worked the camera properly.''

He came to where she stood by the corral fence, and wiped his brow with his rolled-up shirt. ''Was I every photographer's dream come true?'' he asked suggestively. He came closer still and was pleased when she appeared to be affected by his proximity. Her tongue skimmed her lower lip while her eyes scanned his bare chest.

''Oh, you were wonderful,'' she said, nervously fussing with the camera knobs.

''You will let me see the photographs when they're developed, won't you?''

She gazed into his eyes with a distracted look. ''Oh, you'll see them all right.''

"Good." Unable to stop himself, he took a lock of her hair and ran it between his fingers. He'd forgotten just how soft it felt, how fresh it smelled.

"Well," she said, stepping back slightly. "While you're getting your shower, I'll take these into town to get printed."

Shower? He'd just had a shower. "Isn't it a little late for that?" he asked, losing his train of thought. "After all, it's six o'clock on a Monday night. Can't you take them in tomorrow?"

"Oh, no. I need them before that," she said quickly. Her tone softened and she chuckled lightly. "That is, I can't wait to see them. I'll take them in to town and find a place that'll do them right away."

"I'm not sure you will," he argued. "This isn't California, Toots. We don't have twenty-four-hour everything here."

"It's okay, I'll find a place. John will—"

"John will what?"

She edged slightly away. "John will be able to tell me of a place that will do it."

"Well at least wait for me. I'll wash up and drive you in to town. Maybe we can go for supper somewhere."

"No, no. I can't. I have to finish up a couple of articles that need to be in the mail tomorrow. Besides, I'm, uh..."

"Meeting John?" he asked brusquely.

She nodded.

"Fine," he said, stepping back. "Why didn't you just say you had a date, instead of leading me on?"

"Leading you on? But that's not—"

"Never mind," he interrupted, wiping his torso with his shirt. "I get the picture."

She smiled, almost wistfully. "No, you don't." Her voice, soft and low, floated over the evening air. "But you will."

She said goodbye and left. Richard, hot and irritated, scanned her retreating figure. Damn! He hadn't known that she'd been seeing John. When had all this started, and just how serious was it? He'd thought that, despite their disagreement over his father, he and Lesley had been getting along relatively well. Had he been reading more into their relationship than was there? Obviously. Funny, but Lesley didn't strike him as the sort of girl who dated more than one man at the same time. But then, he'd never asked her for a date, so how could he say that he and Lesley were dating?

He wiped his chest with his shirt again. Maybe they should start.

His frown darkened as he watched Lesley swing into Mae's sedan and drive off. With his luck, she'd not only be meeting John tonight, but joining him in his darkroom to see what developed when he regretfully told Lesley that there were no photo stores open.

Richard cursed roundly, slapping the corral rail and making the horses scatter. He cursed John. He cursed photography. And he cursed the day he'd met Lesley even as he wondered where he was destined to end up now that he had.

Lesley stared deep into Richard's eyes. Pale green and hawklike in their intensity, they bore into her soul with the fierceness of a branding iron. His dark brown hair flopped rakishly over his brow, catching the sunlight and reflecting it back. His lips were closed in an expression that connoted neither anger nor happiness.

Lesley's pulse raced as she scanned the column of his neck, skimmed her finger along the broad line of his bare and glistening shoulder, then traced the rippling muscles of his torso. Her breathing became ragged as she imagined his loving hands against her body, then quickened as she pictured her greedy ones on his. The button on his jeans lay undone, teasing her with promises of what lay behind the metal zipper. . . .

"You finished with that photo, honey, or you wanna slobber on it some more?"

Lesley jerked back in her office chair. "Mae, you old dragon," she gasped, tossing her a playfully black glare. "I was just checking to make sure it's the right one for the cover."

"Of course it's the right one," Mae said, holding it up. She looked over to Lesley who was fussing unnecessarily with the papers on her desk. "You are one lucky girl, d'you know that?"

"I'm not sure I know what you mean," Lesley said vaguely, raising her eyes to Mae's at the sound of her hearty laughter.

"Of course you don't," Mae accused. "But that's beside the point." She tossed a stapled wad of paper down on Lesley's desk. "I came to tell you that that is a really fine piece of writing. It's warm, funny and describes our Bucky perfectly. And you wrote it in less than a day. Tell me, where'd you get the background information so fast?"

"His dad. He was more than happy to help. He'd just had another argument with Richard about moving, and said that he'd love to be included in anything that would keep his son out of his hair." She frowned slightly. "Are you sure this plan is going to work?"

"Oh, it'll work all right," Mae assured her. "Question is, do you *want* it to?"

"What do you mean?"

Mae plopped down into the chair opposite Lesley's desk and steepled her fingers. "When this magazine hits the stands, Buck's gonna have women phoning and writing like crazy. Are you sure that's what you want?"

Lesley trained her features into her best nonchalant look. "It makes no difference to me," she said firmly. "All I want is to keep him busy and out of our lives. What better way than to put his advertisement in the magazine and find him a girlfriend? It's perfect. It's exactly what I want."

Mae studied her for several moments, then shrugged and stood up. "As long as you're sure."

"Of course I am. When will the first copy be ready?"

"If you take this stuff over right now, it'll be ready in no time. I've called in a favor from the printer. He'll have to work like a dog, but he's assured me he'll have a hundred advance copies done by Friday, and the rest by deadline."

"How do you know he's dependable?"

Mae smiled wisely. "Because he won't get the two lemon meringue pies I promised if he lets me down."

Lesley laughed loudly and watched a cocky Mae waltz back to her office with an extra large cup of coffee and a maple iced donut. Still chuckling, Lesley slid the article into a brown manila envelope and rose, her eyes catching the glossy eight-by-ten photograph of Richard.

Her fingers automatically traced the shape of his face.

Was she sure? she asked herself for the hundredth time. Was she beyond-a-shadow-of-a-doubt sure that she wanted every woman in the state and beyond to know that Richard Conway was single and eligible? What if one of the women who answered his advertisement was the right woman for him? How would she feel then?

Lesley wavered, teetering on the brink of telling Mae not to use Richard's article after all. But why? Because she was falling for the man herself? The very thought overwhelmed her, making her feel weak and dependent. Fight it, Lesley, she told herself. Think of something else, such as ten good reasons to push on with the article and find Richard a girlfriend to keep him occupied.

Without much thought, ten good reasons came to mind, among them, revenge for his ridiculous Alaskan coral snake story. Lesley felt her cheeks burn. When eight pairs of laughing eyes had turned to her over the dinner table, she'd wanted to be swallowed up and never heard from again. Only the thought that one day she'd repay Richard in kind had kept her sane.

She felt her determination return. Oh yes, she told herself firmly. She slid the picture into the envelope and sealed it shut. This was exactly what she wanted. And with a nod to Mae through her glass walls, Lesley grabbed her purse and headed for the printer's shop.

It wasn't working. Richard pulled up in front of Conway House and turned off the ignition. He'd flown a group of Japanese tourists to the far corners of the state for six days this time, but as much as he loved flying, his thoughts had been firmly fixed on the end of the tour and coming home.

To Lesley.

He opened the heavy front door and was greeted by a noisy, bouncing Wolf whom he quietened with a rough pat on the head. Before he could say anything to the animal, however, it had disappeared through the doorway into the lounge.

Richard peered in and was amazed to see Wolf jump up onto one of the sofas and nestle close to Lesley who sat reading a newsmagazine.

"Richard," she said, smiling as she sat up straight.

He warmed to the sight of her and wondered if it was surprise or pleasure lighting up her features.

"How's it going?" he asked, taking a seat on the opposite sofa. He nodded toward Wolf. "Looks like you made a friend while I was gone."

She looked at the dog panting by her side and she chuckled. "It would seem that way." She turned back to Richard. "How's everything with you?"

He hesitated, wondering if he should broach the plans that had crowded his head these past days. Something told him not to. It was too soon. A lot still had to be arranged, and he didn't want to get anybody's hopes up with plans that didn't work out after all.

"Fine," he said instead. He took a deep breath and decided there was no time like the present to break a promise he wanted more than anything to keep. "Fine, except that I won't be able to take you to the cabin tomorrow after all."

"Oh," she said quietly. "Oh. That's okay."

"No, it's not okay," he snapped. He'd agreed a week ago that he'd take her to the cabin to gather notes on life in the backwoods. The series of articles she was writing was important to her, and he hated like hell to let her down. But then unforeseen changes and cancellations were going to figure highly in the new regime, he reminded himself. So would disappointing those close to him.

"I understand, really." She smiled warmly, but he could tell her heart wasn't in it. Damn, he felt like a heel.

"It's business. If it was anything else, I'd change my plans."

Lesley shifted slightly, sliding her arm around Wolf and scratching his neck. "Richard, I said I understand. Don't make a big deal out of it. Maybe we can go when you get back."

Richard frowned and shook his head. Why did Lesley have to be so understanding? It always made him feel worse when someone took bad news well. He'd rather she got angry, maybe give him the cold shoulder, anything that would make him feel less of a louse.

Running a quick mental check, he considered the million and one things he'd wanted to accomplish before leaving tomorrow. Half an hour now and dinner later was all the time he'd allotted to spend at the house. Still, he wondered, watching Lesley stroke Wolf's silver fur, what was more important? A well-prepared trip, or time with Lesley?

"What I meant to say," he said, catching her eyes, "is that I can't go tomorrow, but I can take you right now."

She flashed a bright smile, telling him that he'd made the right decision. "Really? Great. I'll go get my things and be right back."

She'd jumped up and disappeared before he had a chance to tell her that he'd had a long, rough morning and would like a shower and a shave before heading out. He dragged a palm along his cheek. Oh, well, like everything else, it could wait. Making Lesley happy was more important.

She returned five minutes later with a smile and a pad of paper and a pen that she tucked into her jumpsuit breast pocket.

"A good reporter always comes prepared," she said, with mock solemnity. "And I am a good reporter." She fell into step beside him as they made their way out the front door and headed for the barn. "I intend to be a *great* reporter someday, but that takes time."

Richard slipped a hand around her shoulders. "You'll make it, Toots."

"Think so?"

"I know so," he assured her.

And he did. If anything had become clear over the past weeks, it was that Lesley was a truly special woman meant for great things. Honest and sincere, she'd proven to be a remarkably hard worker, both at the boardinghouse and at the magazine. She rarely lost her cool and seemed to be popular with everyone. Unfortunately, that included the male guests at Conway House. Although she seemed to treat them with distant respect, Richard knew that one day someone special would come along and sweep her off her feet.

Then he'd have lost his chance with her. He ran his palms along his thighs and grabbed a snaffle bit from a nail on the barn wall. Not that it mattered much now. If the plans he was making went through, he wouldn't have anything to offer Lesley anyway, and she'd be better off without him.

He watched her stroke the mare's soft nose and felt his heart contract.

Lesley might be better off without him, but how the hell was he going to make it without her?

Chapter Six

Lesley peered out the cabin's tiny kitchen window with dismay.

"That's the bathroom?" The only other time she'd been at the cabin, the subject of facilities had been the last thing on her mind. Now that she was spending the day in the backwoods, however, it seemed rather significant that there was no indoor plumbing. She took a better look at the tiny, ramshackle outhouse that held the facilities, such as they were. The building was made of gunmetal gray corrugated tin with a shingle roof that looked ready to blow off. In fact, the whole thing looked ready to fall over at any minute. "Good Lord," she said wryly. "Just how primitive does it get up here?"

"Pretty darn primitive, Cheechako," Richard replied, laughing as he teased her with the native word for a newcomer to Alaska.

She grinned in return. "Okay, okay. I'll try harder." She turned away from the window and leaned against the chipped countertop. "But I had no idea this reporting business would require such sacrifices."

"Take it from me, Toots. You never get anywhere in life without sacrifices." Richard carefully poured boiling water from the blackened kettle into two mugs of instant coffee, stirring the contents briskly, then adding sugar and dried creamer. "There you go," he said, handing her one.

She took it from him. "Well, sacrifices aside, is there anything else I should know about before we go any further?"

He shook his head. "Not that I can think of. Other than to watch for insects when you sit down in the outhouse, and calmly back away from any bear you might run into on the way back to the cabin."

Lesley felt her stomach drop a mile and sent Richard a look that begged him to admit he was joking. But he'd turned away to wipe down the counter and had his back to her. She could see his shoulders moving beneath the chambray of his shirt but couldn't tell if he was laughing or coughing. She wrapped her arms about herself for moral protection and scanned the cabin's main room.

It was just as she remembered it, warm and folksy, with a distinct, woodsy smell that no doubt came from the strapping log walls and wood strip floor. Even the vaulted ceiling had been lined with cedar.

"Actually, there is something I want you to promise me," he admitted, coming up behind her. She turned and fought the urge to nestle close. "Don't ever, for any reason, wander off into the bush without me. You may not come out again, and I'd hate to lose you."

Lesley shuddered. This was too much for her and her middle-class California upbringing. She nodded in agreement and vowed never to take running water and toilets for granted again.

"Hey—" Richard chuckled, putting her mug on the table before wrapping her in his arms "—I didn't mean to scare you." She laid her hands against his waist and felt instantly comforted. "There are just certain rules that are better observed than ignored." He smoothed a hand across her shoulders and looked down into her face. "It's a matter of survival."

Survival, Lesley mused silently, watching in slow motion as his lips descended upon hers. She tilted her head back slightly, greedy and impatient for the taste of him. It had been a long, lonely six days. She wondered—no, hoped—that he'd suffered the same aching desire that had kept her awake these past nights.

His kiss deepened, and she knew he had.

This is crazy, she thought, winding her arms about Richard's trim waist and sliding them along his back. The fabric of his shirt stood between her and his skin, frustrating her. She considered, in her desirous stupor, pulling the shirt from his waistband, but before she could, he drew back.

Blatant desire glittered in his eyes. She matched it until he drew a deep breath and released her.

"I'd better get some wood," he said, turning abruptly.

The cabin door rattled on rusty hinges as it closed behind him, leaving the cabin suddenly cold and empty. Lesley crossed to the side window. Richard was heading for the tree stump and the woodpile, stripping off his shirt as he went. He tossed the garment onto the pile of logs, then grabbed a log and placed it end up on the stump.

His arms raised the ax high in the air and brought it down with an almighty wallop, easily splitting the log in two. He threw the pieces aside and grabbed another log. And another. He was either extremely industrious or had a lot of tension to work off. Lesley hoped it was the impact of their kiss that was testing his patience as a gentleman.

Lesley's fingers came to her mouth, gently skimming her lower lip.

Why had he pulled back so quickly? What had suddenly occurred to him to make him withdraw from their embrace? A sudden guilty streak? Honor? Or...maybe a girlfriend he'd been visiting on his recent trip?

Lesley watched as he continued to split logs as though his life depended on it. His bronzed sweat-glazed back shone in the sunlight. The muscles of his arms were firm and well exercised, his forearms lightly coated with fine dark hair. A sprinkling of the same coated his broad chest, trickling downward until it disappeared beneath the waistband of his jeans. Lesley sighed appreciatively. A finer physical specimen she had never seen, and she'd seen a couple in her twenty-five years.

But Richard's appeal was more complex than that. Much as she'd tried to deny any feelings for him, she was attracted to his concern for his father, his love of the outdoors, the teasing word he always had for Mae.

It was no wonder she was so drawn to him. She slid her hands into her pockets and laughed ruefully. There had been a time, not so long ago, that the very thought would have sent her running for the nearest airport. Now she simply accepted her affection for Richard as something that had been inevitable from the start.

Not that anything would come of it, she reminded herself. They each had their own lives and their own roads to follow. And although Richard seemed to have his life pretty much on track, she couldn't imagine where she was destined to end up at the end of her stay in Alaska.

That thought, which not long ago had excited her, now scared her half to death. Not because she was incapable of making it on her own but because no matter where she moved, Richard wouldn't be there... unless she chose Los Angeles. But then that would look as if she were chasing him, and she was too proud to appear desperate.

Besides, she thought with a sudden angry pang of jealousy, he'd once admitted that he had his choice of women back in California. Probably a dozen or more just waiting by the phone. Waiting and praying that the almighty Richard Conway would call, looking for a date.

Well, Lesley thought hotly, they were welcome to him. There was no way she was going to become one of his groupies. Why, he'd just have to—

Lesley listened to herself and broke out into ironic laughter. She sounded like a jealous girlfriend, she thought wryly. She laid her palms on her cheeks and shook her head. Richard had been right to pull back. There was nowhere for their relationship to go other than to evolve into a casual summer affair with both parties saying goodbye at the end of August.

It was too heartbreaking a scenario to consider. Silently, Lesley thanked Richard for the foresight to back off. If he hadn't, she might have made a huge fool of herself by showing how much she cared, when, for all she knew, Richard wouldn't remember her name by the end of the summer.

What a shame, she thought sadly, *when I'll remember every little detail about you until time stands still.*

"Damned-awful horses," Richard growled, slamming the cabin door closed with his foot and tossing the wood down into a pile by the tiny fireplace.

"What's wrong with the horses?" Lesley asked, looking up from her armchair. She'd curled up with a blanket just after supper when the weather had turned cool.

"Alaskan horses," he explained, crouching down before the fireplace grate. He crumpled up a piece of old newspaper and covered it with kindling before laying two heavier logs on top. "Mosquitoes, to you outsiders," he explained, stopping to scratch his arm. He dragged a box of long matches from the mantel, lit the fire and stood back up. "There. That should warm it up in here. How about a drink of brandy? Would that help?"

She nodded, and he went into the kitchen, pulling down the dusty bottle and searching out two glasses. All he could find were juice glasses decorated with teddy bears.

Great. Impress her with your class.

"Best I can do," he said wryly, handing her one.

"It's fine." She stuck her hand out from under the quilt to take the glass. One sip, and she smacked her lips inelegantly. "Whew! That's powerful stuff."

"I only use it for medicinal purposes, you understand," he teased, sitting on the floor and propping himself against the coffee table by her feet.

He lifted his gaze and marveled again at Lesley's simple beauty. The golden light of the fire bathed her face in a warm glow that softened her smile and made her appear breathtakingly innocent. A log on the fire shifted, then crackled and popped with a fiery show of sparks. The only other sounds were the ticking of an old regulator clock on the wall and the scratching of a bush against one of the windows.

"Tired?" he asked, when her eyes drifted shut and she leaned her head back.

She smiled and turned her face toward him. "Thinking," she answered drowsily. "About how perfect this day's been and how much I love it here in Alaska."

"Did you learn a lot today?" he asked, knowing she'd taken enough notes to choke both horses outside. When she'd run out of scratch pad, she'd actually resorted to scribbling on paper towels.

Lesley took a long, slow sip of her drink and licked her lips. Richard watched her tongue's journey with envy.

"Bucky, you wouldn't believe what I've learned today."

"Glad to be of service." She gave him a slightly odd smile then took another sip of her drink. "Be careful. This is pretty strong stuff."

"What's the matter? Afraid I'll get drunk and make a pass?" she said with a carefree laugh.

He smiled lewdly. "One can always hope."

She laughed again, then held out her glass to him. "Here. Maybe you'd better take it after all. I'm getting silly, and I don't know why." She stretched, then pulled the blanket back around her shoulders. "All that exercise today made me tired, I guess."

"You call one twenty-minute horseback ride and a full day of relaxing on the porch, exercise?"

"Yes, I do," she replied with mock-severity. She sighed dreamily. "Sometimes I consider getting up in the morning more exercise than I care to do."

"What you need is a good reason for getting out of bed," he said, standing to prod the fire, "or an even better one for staying *in* it." *Like making love until noon, then starting all over again.*

Richard took a seat on the coffee table and wondered if it was the heat from the fire or his innuendo that was causing Lesley's cheeks to pinken. She'd lowered her gaze to the scratchy plaid blanket and was plucking at the torn binding along the edge. If he didn't know better, he'd say he'd embarrassed her. Pretty commendable, considering just how much it took to rattle her cage.

"Don't listen to me," he said casually. He leaned back on his hands and stretched his legs out in front of him, hooking one ankle over the other. "I'm just rambling."

"I don't mind. But I am curious. I mean, as far as cheechakos go, how did I do today? Would you at least give me honorable mention for making it through the day without killing us both?"

He almost laughed at the hopeful look in her eyes. "Oh, sure. Anybody who can burn macaroni on a hot plate gets full marks in my book."

She blushed. "Yes, well, I told you I wasn't a good cook."

"What *are* you good at, then?"

She pursed her lips. "Not much, really. I'm a lousy cook, I hate housework and I'm basically lazy."

Richard tried to think of something appropriate to say. He knew she was far from lazy, although she was easily one of the worst damned cooks he'd ever run into.

"And your good points?" he asked with a doubtful grin.

She smiled instantly. "I know how to short sheet a bed when I need to."

"Don't I know it?" he said wryly. "It took me fifteen minutes to unscrew my bed that night. My butt was freezing by the time I got under the covers." He smiled suggestively. "I sleep in the raw, in case you were wondering."

"I wasn't," she said a little too quickly. She held out her hand. "Maybe I'd better have that brandy after all." She laughed roundly. "I need fortification. This day—never mind the summer—isn't turning out at all like I figured."

He gave her glass back. "What were you expecting when you came to Alaska?"

"Well, I guess I thought I'd get to keep my own name. So far I've been christened Toots, hon and darlin'. I'm being plagued by a man called Buck, and I keep company with a dog called Wolf and two cats named Ping and Pong." She gave him a look of complete incredulity. "Doesn't *anyone* around here have a normal name and do normal things?"

"That depends," he answered slowly. He swirled the golden liquid around in his juice glass and looked at her with the intensity a psychiatrist would show one of his more interesting patients. "What does normal mean to you?"

She grinned back. "Well, I may be old-fashioned, but normal to me does not include wild moose walking the streets of downtown, and hints on how to out-logic a bear on the way back from the outhouse." She grimaced. "Speaking of which, I think I need to use your facilities."

"Right this way," he said, standing and offering her his arm.

Early evening had settled in dim and cool, although it was not yet late. They'd have to be getting back soon, or risk being eaten alive by the mosquitoes. Richard escorted Lesley to the outhouse, taking her blanket as he opened the door, then wandering several polite steps away as he considered which of his jackets to give her for the ride back to the big house. He'd no sooner propped his foot on a fallen tree when a bloodcurdling shriek rent the quiet night air.

He covered the short distance to the outhouse in a flash, but she was already outside, her face pale and her hands dragging the blanket from a nearby branch. She wrapped it around herself.

"There's a . . . a . . . *thing* in there," she rasped.

"There's probably a lot of things in there," he said gently, fighting the urge to take her in his arms. "Do you want me to investigate?" he asked, surprised when she only nodded in reply to his teasing tone.

She must really be spooked, he thought, entering the outhouse and brushing away the insect she'd no doubt viewed as the Loch Ness monster. He emerged with a serious frown, to keep from breaking into a grin, and nodded.

"It's ready for you now."

She crept forward, peering inside as he held the door open. "Don't go away."

"Wouldn't dream of it."

He frowned and bit the inside of his lip, almost drawing blood as she entered and exited in what had to be a record time.

It was all he could do to keep a straight face. "I need more wood," he said somberly. "You go back to the cabin, okay?"

She nodded and took off like a rabbit outrunning a fox, her blanket dragging every twig, leaf and doggie chew stick beneath it as she went. The last thing they needed was more wood, yet Richard had jumped on the flimsy excuse to keep him outside and occupied where he could have a good laugh and not hurt Lesley's feelings.

Less than five minutes later, he felt he had himself under control and returned to the cabin where Lesley stood over the kitchen sink, rinsing out their juice glasses.

Allowing her the first word, he immediately went over to the fireplace and stirred the dying embers in the grate. There was no point in putting any more logs on, both because they'd be leaving soon and because enough heat and golden light still emanated from the smoldering fire.

Busy studying the few last flames, he didn't notice Lesley come up behind him. He turned and smiled at her sheepish grin.

"I'm not doing too well, am I?" she said.

"You're okay. You need to toughen up a bit, but for a city slicker, I'd say you're doing pretty good."

"You're just being nice. I think I'm the biggest failure this area's seen in years."

She arched her back, but grimaced when she tilted her head to the side.

"What's wrong?"

"My neck hurts," she replied, rubbing it with the palm of her hand. "It feels like it's been pushed three steps to the left."

"That could be because you're not used to riding," Richard admitted. "Although it could also have been that flying leap you took through the outhouse door." He caught her chiding grin. "Sorry." To make amends, he pulled the tattered plaid footstool in front of the fire. "Here. Sit down. I'll give you a neck rub. That might help."

He lowered Lesley down, positioned himself behind her, and gently but firmly, began to knead the muscles of her shoulders through the wrinkled fabric of her jumpsuit.

"Feel good?" he asked. She sighed and made a little moaning sound of contentment. "Here," he said, reaching forward and undoing the top two buttons of her suit. "Let's do this. It'll feel even better." He felt her stiffen when his hands pushed aside the fabric and slid along her skin, then relax again when he began easing the tension from her neck.

Her skin was satin beneath his palms—silky, smooth and warm. He caressed her neck, pleased when she bent her head forward to allow him access. His pulse was beginning to respond, as were other things. Brushing aside her tousled hair, he leaned down and kissed the soft point on her neck just below her ear.

"Oh!" she said, jumping slightly.

"Relax," he whispered. "It's all part of the treatment."

"Treatment for what?"

"Whatever ails ya'."

"But nothing hurts."

"Maybe not from where you're sitting," he muttered, letting his hands roam farther with every sweep. He pushed the thought from his mind and forced his voice to sound controlled. "I know these things. They don't call me Dr. Buck for nothing."

She sighed but said nothing, simply leaned back and rested against Richard's body. He felt himself arch to meet her, but if she noticed his arousal, she said nothing. She was completely tranquil, her breathing calm and even and her hands clasped loosely in her lap. Fueled by her acceptance of his hands on her body, he slid his palms down her chest and opened another button on her jumpsuit.

Another slight moan. Swallowing hard to maintain some semblance of self-control, he skimmed the top of Lesley's breasts, which were sheathed in a flimsy pink lace bra. Another button undone and her suit was open to the waist. His hands shook slightly as he pushed it aside completely. Her head, resting against his midsection, drifted back and forth in languorous, fluid movements silently granting him permission to continue.

He looked down, scanning Lesley's body and admiring its perfection. Gently but firmly, he watched his hands push aside the lacy bra and allow her breasts to spill over the edges. The throbbing in his groin told him to stop now, while he could, but Lesley's acquiescence urged him on. He'd never been this close to her before, and he'd be damned if he was going to forfeit the opportunity now.

She sighed dreamily, and he watched her breasts rise and fall. Before he knew it himself, he'd slid his hands downward and cupped one in each hand, extracting from her a slow, breathy groan of pleasure. She was heavy in his hand, silken and smooth, and he caressed her with the same care he'd show anything precious. His whispered name filled the air as he bent down and laved her neck with warm kisses.

"Damn, Lesley," he said sharply. "You're so beautiful . . . I want you so much."

He felt her ease that little bit closer to him, and knew that the moment they'd been powerless to avoid was upon them. Five steps and they'd be in the bedroom, naked on his lonely king-size bed, entwined as they were meant to be, as he fulfilled every one of Lesley's wildest fantasies. Urgency filled his body, making it tight and demanding.

Hell. Forget the bed. The footstool would do. He could be stripped in seconds and sitting where she was now. Her clothes were already half off. He'd help her with what little remained, then pull her down on top of him. An even hotter surge of desire coiled in his gut. If he did that, Lesley's breasts would be right where he'd want them. Close enough to taste. His touch would send her into a frenzy, and she'd wind her fingers through his hair and call out his name as he brought her to a peak she'd only ever dreamed of.

The fantasy was more than any normal man could ignore, and Richard was no exception. He needed to get out of there.

He took a calming breath but it was a useless exercise. He was too far gone for common sense. He thought again about the bed in the next room, and pictured this woman, his woman, smiling and sated from a long night of loving. She'd open her arms to him, and he'd join her again, and so it would go every day and night from then on. . . .

Sudden anger surged through Richard's body, filling the recesses that had moments ago housed desire. What the hell did he think he was doing? Lesley was not his woman. He had no right to take her physically without even the vaguest emotional commitment. And the way his life was heading, he couldn't give her that.

Richard slowly withdrew, pulling Lesley's jumpsuit closed across her breasts and clenching his hands into tense fists. He took a step back to distance himself, praying that he'd stopped in time. He'd been around enough to have suffered emotional involvements before. Some hurt, some didn't. This one would hurt like a son of a bitch.

Several tension-filled seconds passed before Lesley turned and looked up at him.

"Richard?" she asked, her eyes filled with confusion.

The words of love that had filled his thoughts mere moments ago were gone now. Only the harsh reality that he'd almost allowed their relationship to go one step further and hurt a woman he cared very much for, remained.

"Did I do something wrong?" she asked, holding her suit together with shaky hands. "If I did, I'm sorry—"

"No," he butted in. "You didn't do anything wrong." He crossed to the fireplace and leaned on the mantel, his hand automatically rubbing the back of his neck as he gave her time to do up her buttons. Several more seconds passed.

Man, that was close, he thought tersely. Only guilt that Lesley deserved better had given him the strength to call a halt to what would no doubt have been the biggest mistake of their relationship. Not only did she deserve complete honesty, she also deserved promises and a future. Time to explore her career, and the freedom to follow it and see where it took her.

He sighed tersely and flexed his fingers. She deserved all the things he couldn't give her right now because he'd taken her advice and made plans for his father to keep the boardinghouse. He shook his head. In giving Lesley what she'd wanted, he'd been forced to let her go.

He ached to tell her the truth behind his withdrawal, but it was still too soon. Nothing was close to being finalized yet. And because he couldn't explain his actions, he knew she was probably feeling pretty confused and hurt right about now.

He returned to her, tempering the frustrations in his voice as he gently stroked her arms. "You must know that I think you're a beautiful, desirable woman. One I would really love to take into that bedroom and not let out of my sight for a week."

But? her eyes asked.

"But that wouldn't be a smart thing for us to do." He scanned her features. "Not when a couple of weeks might be all I can give you."

Lesley's entire body stiffened. "I understand," she whispered, tersely trying to pull from his grasp. And she did understand. Perfectly. She'd been given the brush-off before. She recognized that look in a man's eye that told her goodbye and good luck. Although to be fair, it had usually been right after an evening spent with her family. This time she had no one but herself to blame for an evening gone wrong.

She'd been too forward, she told herself, too eager. Too obvious. She cringed inwardly. Oh, Lord, had she been so obvious that he'd realized the depth of her

feelings and been scared off? How absolutely morti-
fying if he'd realized that she'd come to care for him
and received, instead of a casual evening of passion,
the fright of his life.

"Lesley," he said lowly, pulling her thoughts back.
"I know I'm not saying the right things here. But I'm
not good at this."

But I am. From deep within her bag of facades,
Lesley pulled her most frequently used: that of a cool,
calm, in-control woman of the nineties. Almost automatically, her shoulders braced, her voice became
well modulated and her embarrassed frown melted
into an understanding smile.

"Richard, for heaven's sake," she said breezily.
"Don't worry about it. In fact, just forget about it all
together."

"But—"

"Honest. No buts," she said, laughing with a confidence she didn't feel. "This was just one of those
embarrassing situations that happens when two people start relaxing a little too much, have a little too
much to drink—"

"I didn't drink too much—"

"Well, I did," she said, waving away his words.
"And now I'm feeling pretty silly, so...can we just
forget about it and go home?"

She watched a stiff, cold mask of his own descend
upon Richard's face and wondered what she'd said to
make him angry. After all, he'd been the one to pull
back, not her. Maybe he'd wanted to make some macho speech about his own self-righteousness when
she'd taken the wind out of his sails. Well, regardless,
what was done was done, and she'd meant it when
she'd said that the whole episode was best forgotten.

Richard made some grunting noises, most likely to show his irritation, and vigorously stirred the dying embers.

"Let's go," he said finally, standing back up.

He didn't take her arm but did open the cabin door for her. Funny, but she missed even the touch of his guiding hand on her elbow. It wasn't much, but it was something.

"You and I will ride back on Caesar," he said brusquely.

Lesley shot him a surprised stare, but didn't argue. He must have his reasons. Maybe Lizzy was tired, or lame. It didn't matter. She didn't know a thing about horses, and had little choice but to follow Richard's orders.

Richard helped Lesley onto Caesar's bare back, then swung up behind her. His arms about her waist, he held the reins loosely and clicked his teeth. Caesar moved ahead, turning to go down the forest path, while an obedient Lizzy followed close behind.

"Won't she run off?" Lesley asked, fighting to keep her thoughts on something other than the effect of Richard's closeness. She could feel his warmth through the flannel shirt he'd slipped on her as they'd left the cabin. His scent permeated the rough fabric, assailing her senses and making her heartbeat quicken. Pushed back against his chest as Caesar rocked beneath them, Lesley could feel the tenseness in Richard's body.

"No, she won't," he said abruptly.

Lesley sighed and tried to relax, but it was difficult. Richard's terseness was a sign that he was still upset. A heavy sigh escaped her as she tried to sit upright on Caesar's glossy black back. Maybe if she wasn't actually touching Richard, she'd be able to forget his gentle touch and how it had—

"Relax," he growled, sliding a hand to her stomach and pulling her back. She could hardly refuse with his hand wrapped around her waist. "You'll make your neck worse if you don't."

Lesley could believe it, and tried to loosen the muscles threatening to snap her in two. She'd almost accomplished it when Richard's hand slipped beneath the oversize shirt and nestled against the fabric of her jumpsuit.

She caught her breath, then released it as casually as possible. She'd give anything to know what Richard was feeling right now. Was he irritated by what had happened back at the cabin? Or just frustrated that, for whatever reason, they hadn't ended up in bed?

A sickly shiver raced through Lesley. If he was angry over something like that, how upset was he going to be when he saw his picture on the cover of *Northern Man Monthly?*

She dismissed the possibilities as too horrific to contemplate, reminding herself that the release date was still almost two weeks away. Surely in that length of time, she'd be able to think up some logical excuse as to why she'd taken liberties with his personal life.

Lesley bit her lip until it hurt. Two short weeks.

If I caught a plane tomorrow, how far away from Anchorage could I be by then... ?

Chapter Seven

Richard heaved a large paper-wrapped bundle of magazines down on the floor beside the store till and smiled at the pretty woman behind the counter. "There you go, Jackie. The new *Northern Man Monthly*. Hot off the press."

"Great!" she said, bending to slice open the brown wrapping. "Thanks for bringing them early. I've been waiting weeks for this issue. Word is, they got someone really special for the cover—"

The woman stood back up, her bright smile fading into stunned disbelief.

"What's wrong, Jackie? Seen a ghost?"

She seemed to be struggling for words. "Why didn't you say something?" she asked finally. "I've heard of secrets, but . . ." She held up a copy of the magazine.

It was Richard's turn to lose color. "What the hell . . . ?" he grunted, grabbing it from her. "What kind of a joke—"

"No joke," Jackie said, dragging another copy from the bundle and flipping to the center page. She held it up lengthwise and whistled. "Nice pectorals, Rich. See?" she said, showing him the photograph. "This is where they put the article for the cover bachelor. And this month, Rich, you're *it!*"

"The hell I am," he spat, flipping to the middle of the magazine and reading his own biography. "Born... raised... aw, jeez!" he said, his face crinkling in disbelief. "They've even put a mailing address in here."

"Who's *they,* do you think?"

Richard's eyes narrowed. "Laurel and Hardy."

"Translated?"

He looked her in the eye, and she took a step back. "The two women who have dogged my every step for the past two months. Just wait until I get my hands on them!"

He left the store without another word, his hands twisted around the double issue of *Northern Man Monthly.*

"No charge!" Jackie called out after him, but he didn't hear.

Richard's first stop was the *Northern Man* office, but as he'd suspected, Mae and Lesley were nowhere to be found. And if the receptionist knew but wasn't saying where they were, then she deserved an Academy Award for Best Supporting Actress.

Richard's truck, when pushed to the limit, was a capable vehicle, and he was soon pulling up in front of Conway House in a noisy cloud of dust. Mae's European sedan was parked on the perimeter of the small gravel parking area, proof that she was somewhere in the area. And if she was, no doubt her side-kick would be hiding in a cupboard close by.

He stormed the porch steps, magazine in hand, ready to tear the house apart, but he found not only Mae and Lesley enjoying midmorning coffee in the lounge but his father also. A fire crackled in the grate of the lava-stone fireplace, filling the room with the heavy smell of wood smoke. Over in the corner, two guests sat hunched over the chess table, transfixed by their game. And Wolf, the traitor, sat by Lesley's feet.

One of the guests looked up. "Hot stuff, Rich!" he called over, then returned to the game and his opponent, who waved absently.

Richard's eyes zeroed in on the cozy group clustered around the main coffee table. Coming close, he flipped open the magazine and held up his half-naked photograph.

"Like it, hon?" Mae said brazenly. "I think it's a great picture. Don't you, Bob?"

"Oh, I like it a lot. In fact, I was just sayin' to Lesley, here, that—"

"Explain!" He tossed the magazine on the table, and jammed his hands on his hips.

"Explain what?" Mae asked. "We needed someone for the cover. You're a man, you're still single and you're still breathing. You qualified."

"Don't you think it would've been nice to *ask* first?"

"Of course not," she answered. "You'd have said no."

"Damn right, I would've." Richard took a deep, calming breath and ran a hand along the back of his neck. This conversation definitely wasn't going the way he'd expected. Actually, he'd been expecting to find both women cowering in fear. Sorry, apologetic, visibly shaking beneath the power of his might and fury, possibly even begging for mercy. And what did he get? A morning coffee-and-cookie break, with idle chatter revolving around the one topic of conversation he felt sure they'd want to avoid. Their blatant nonchalance left him stunned, and he sat down next to Lesley.

"You're not even sorry you did it," he said.

"Of course not," she admitted, shifting slightly away from him. "What's to be sorry about? We really were in a bind. And since you're usually such a helpful sort of person, we just naturally assumed you'd be willing to do this one little favor."

Somewhere in the background Mae started to cough. His father, too, although Richard thought nothing of it. His eyes were on Lesley's face, mesmerized by its angelic innocence, while his body enjoyed the same heady wave of attraction that washed over him whenever they were together.

"Well," he said, with a low chuckle. "Since you put it that way...."

"I knew you'd be reasonable." She laid a hand on his thigh. "Thank you so much."

He wanted to tell her that with her palm warming his body that way, he'd do a lot more than just let her put his picture in a nationwide magazine. Instead, he laid his hand over hers to prolong the contact.

He looked over to his father. "I suppose you gave her the background information."

"I'm not gonna lie," Bob said, tutting. "Yes, son. I did. For all of us."

All of us? "What does that mean?"

"So, Bucky," Mae cut in smoothly. "I think Lesley did a wonderful job on the photography, don't you?"

He switched his attention to Mae, who sat tucked in her favorite corner of the sofa looking like an oversize zebra in her black-and-white-striped dress and matching headband. "Yes, I do. For a beginner, she's very good." He hesitated and tried to catch Lesley's eye but she was tinkering absently with her teacup. "You *are* a beginner, aren't you?" She remained conspicuously silent, so he gently squeezed her thigh. "Tell the truth."

She looked over the table to Bob, then reluctantly turned to Richard.

"Well, I'm no professional, but I guess I do know a few things about film speed and f-stops."

Richard laughed loudly and shook his head. "You guys are crazy—all of you."

"You aren't mad?" Lesley asked tentatively.

"I was at first, but not now." He gave her one of his best smiles and saw her body relax.

"We were 'fraid you'd skin us alive," Bob admitted, sitting back on the opposite sofa.

"Not that it stopped you," Richard said. He peered across to Mae who sat sipping her coffee like a duchess at a garden party. "I'm sure this was all your idea."

"You bet," she said quickly. "All my idea. Good one, at that, don't you think?"

"A doozy, Mae. A real doozy." He slapped his knee and rose. "Well, if you'll excuse me. I've been going since six this morning, and I'm starved. I need something to eat. Don't go away." He looked down into Lesley's sweet face and tapped her nose. "You're hanging out with bad people, Toots. They're leading you into temptation something awful. I'd watch out if I were you."

She smiled but said nothing, and he left the room, whistling as he made his way to the back kitchen. There, he grabbed a cherry Danish off a plate on the counter, ate half and poured himself a glass of milk. Food in hand, he sauntered back down the hall, stopping in the foyer to kick off his boots. As he sat down on the lower step of the staircase, the sound of muffled voices reached him.

"I thought for sure he was gonna..."

"Bob, you almost blew it...."

"...if he found out why we really did it, he'd have our hides on display over the mantel...."

Richard slid from his boots and tried to make sense of the scraps of conversation filtering in from the lounge. But it didn't add up to anything logical until Lesley's earnest whisper struck home.

"...if he found out it was *my* idea...."

Richard jumped to his feet and stormed back into the lounge. Lesley nearly dropped her teacup at his sudden reappearance, and Bob looked as guilty as sin.

"*Your* idea?" he said to Lesley, his voice ominously low.

Her eyes darted everywhere. She licked her lips, and he could almost see the wheels turning in her brain as she tried to think of a suitable answer. Then, as was her style, she simply braced her shoulders, took a deep breath and rose to her feet. She turned to face him—cool, calm and collected. This, he thought proudly, was the Lesley he was most familiar with.

"Yes, it was my idea."

"Am I allowed to ask why you did it?"

"Of course." She cleared her throat. "I did it because you are a meddling busybody."

Richard's jaw dropped. It wasn't what he'd been expecting to hear. Because she thought he was the best candidate, they were running late on the deadline, because he was great looking with a body women would kill for—anything. "A busybody?"

"That's right. You're always butting in. You tried to bully me into leaving here the day I arrived, you tried to scare me with the horses, and—" she looked him squarely in the eye "—you embarrassed me with your Alaskan coral snake story."

And she'd promised to get him back for that, as Richard recalled. He watched his father rise to his feet and tighten his belt a notch around a gradually decreasing potbelly.

"And I did it 'cause you're always buggin' me to sell this place and move away," he said matter-of-factly.

Richard cocked an eyebrow at Mae. "C'mon. You can't tell me that you didn't have a reason, too. Let's hear it."

She sat back in the cushions and smiled coyly. "Just because."

Richard rolled his eyes. "Well, so now you've got my picture in a national magazine. So what? How's that going to change anything?"

"It's gonna get you a girlfriend," Bob said, grabbing his mug from the table and walking past Richard. He nudged his shoulder as he passed. "Someone to keep you busy and out of our hair!"

He left the room and Richard stared at Lesley. "Is that true? Is that the convoluted logic you based this whole ridiculous scheme on?"

"It's not convoluted," Lesley insisted, sitting back down. "It's perfectly logical. It's what you need. It's what we all need."

Her words seemed to lose a little punch near the end, but he took them at face value nonetheless.

"I see," he said, nodding thoughtfully. "So this is what it's come to. My hanging around bugged you so much, you had to find a way to get rid of me."

"Oh, no," Lesley said, sitting forward. "It wasn't so much that—"

"Sure it was," Mae interrupted. "Face it, Buck. You poked your nose into other people's business once too often," she said with a grin. "And, like most busybodies, you got it caught."

But Richard had played psychological games with the best of them and refused to rise to Mae's bait. Instead he decided to change tack and see where the tide took him.

"Actually, now that I think about it, you might be right," he said, taking the seat his father had vacated. A tiny pink packet of artificial sweetener lay on the table where his father's coffee mug had sat. A rush of thanks to whoever was taking such good care of the man flooded through Richard.

"We might?" Lesley's voice was tinged with just enough skepticism to tell him that he was heading in the right direction.

"Sure." He dragged his thoughts back to the conversation. "I mean, consider the facts. I'm a great catch, right?" He looked to Mae for verification, but she was as quiet as a clam, and sat in her corner watching him with hawk eyes and a knowing smile. So he turned to Lesley. "Well, aren't I?"

"I suppose so."

"I mean, I'm well-off financially, I'm interesting and I'm good-looking. You said so yourself, didn't you?"

"I suppose I did."

"I think I have a lot to offer a woman, don't you?" he asked, relaxing into the sofa beside Mae and extending his arm along the back. He crossed his right leg over his left knee and nodded. "Yes, I think I see why you chose me. I'm the best catch any woman's likely to land in this lifetime, right, Toots?"

"I guess."

He leaned forward, all signs of teasing wiped from his face, and caught her eye. "Lesley, I owe you an apology and a great big thank-you." She looked at him as though he'd sprouted two heads. "No, I mean it. I want to thank you for putting that advertisement in the magazine. Truly. I'm in your debt."

Mae started chuckling in the corner, a low, confident laugh that came from deep within her ample bosom.

"You want to thank me?" Lesley echoed.

"You bet. This is the nicest thing anyone's ever done for me. You know, Les," he said, lowering his gaze to his hands. "I think I'm ready to settle down. I've been alone too long. I want a woman to share my life, plan a home with. Maybe even have a few little Ritchies running around my feet." He smiled contentedly. "Yeah, I can see it now, and it looks great." He stared at her meaningfully. "And I've got *you* to thank. You will come to the wedding, won't you?"

Mae choked on her coffee and began to cough.

"Wedding?" Lesley echoed. "Aren't you getting a little ahead of yourself?"

"I don't think so. After all, surely there's someone out there in this great big country of ours who's the perfect girl for me." He chuckled confidently. "Maybe even two or three. Maybe I'll have a hell of a time picking just one. What do you say, Maesy?" he asked, flicking a wry grin in her direction.

Mae wiped a tear from the corner of her eye. "You just might at that, Bucky. You just might at that."

Richard leaned across the coffee table and grasped Lesley's hands. They were cold as ice. "Thank you, Lesley," he said earnestly. "Thank you so much. Who knows? If we have a daughter, we might even name her after you."

That, at least, got a reaction. Lesley stood slowly, her bearing that of a member of the nobility, and braced her shoulders.

"That would be wonderful," she said flatly. "Now, if you'll both excuse me . . . ?"

She left the lounge and seconds later the front door closed quietly. Mae let out a whoop of laughter that would have shot Richard out of his seat, had he not been anticipating it.

"Bucky, you *devil* you," she said between gasps. "You are *bad!*"

"How's that, Mae?" he asked blithely. A smile toyed at his mouth, but he forced it back.

"You know damn fine what I'm talking about." She smiled broadly. "You put that girl through the fires of hell just now."

"But for that to be true, Mae darling, she would have to feel some sort of affection for me." He watched her carefully. "Are you saying that's true?"

But Mae wasn't saying anything and sent Richard a chastising grin.

"One of these days, Bucky," she said with a shake of her head. "One of these days you're going to get exactly what you deserve."

"I'm counting on it, Maesy," he said with a thoughtful glance to the empty doorway. "Stay tuned. I think this is going to get good. *Real* good."

"Now, I rather like this one here," Richard said thoughtfully. "Says she's five foot eight, a hundred and twenty-five pounds, 35-22-34." He pushed the photograph across the table to Lesley. "What do you think?"

Lesley looked at the woman in question and felt an icy finger claw at her heart. It had been the tenth picture he'd shown her that morning. His advertisement had been a resounding success, and only one week after its release, the letters and cards were pouring in.

"Very pretty," she said blandly, returning to her tuna fish sandwich. It tasted like two slabs of cardboard with a mashed sawdust filling.

Richard took a big bite of his own pastrami on rye. "Says here that she likes moonlit walks along the beach, swimming in the nude and making love in unusual places."

"Like Alaska?" Mae snorted, slapping a full mug of coffee down on the table beside him before returning to the kitchen counter.

He looked up at her with surprise. "You don't think she sounds good?"

"She sounds wonderful," the woman agreed. "Almost as perfect as Hilda from Harperville, Fanny from Omaha and—"

"No, you must be thinking of Freda from Omaha. Freda was the one with big, uh . . ."

"Assets," Lesley finished.

"Right. Big assets." Richard took a bite of his sandwich and sighed. "Boy, this is turning out to be a lot more difficult than I thought. I had no idea so many women would answer my ad. Did you, Maesy?"

"Nope," Mae replied. She dragged a huge carving knife through her own sandwich and came to sit at the table. "I had no idea there were that many women out there with such low standards."

She smiled sweetly, and he sneered back. Such levity, Lesley thought, grinding away at her lunch. Their words meant nothing to them, rolled off their tongues like so much fluff in the wind. But their banter hurt Lesley to the quick, for when it was all said and done, Mae would be back at her house with her two cats, Richard would be off flying the wild blue yonder with his new wife, and Lesley, well, she'd be nursing a broken heart and trying to find a reporting job in New Guinea.

Pain sliced through Lesley's heart. If she needed proof of her deep and irrevocable love for Richard Conway, it was arriving daily in the bags of scented mail that filled his post-office box to overflowing. Even she hadn't expected so many women to answer his advertisement. She cursed herself for doing such a good job on the article's photography, then raked herself over the coals for describing in words the warm and loving man beneath the virile exterior.

"Oh, jeez," she heard Richard say. He whistled appreciatively. "Now here's a real honey." He shuddered and held up a glossy photo of a young woman, clad in a scanty bikini, reclining on the rocks by a sunny beach. "What do you think?"

Lesley took a swig of milk to force her lunch down her throat. "She's okay," she said peevishly.

"Says her name is Sumi…she lives in Honolulu and is part Tahitian. Oh, yes." He nodded. "*She's* a pretty one."

Mae grabbed the picture and sucked on a back tooth. "Hmm, looks a bit—"

"Doesn't she, though," he butted in, grabbing the picture back. "Her letter also says she's in university studying microbiology, enjoys volunteer work with handicapped children and is an active member of her local Greenpeace organization. Wow!"

"Yeah, but can she whistle Dixie with a mouthful of crackers?"

"Sour grapes, Mae," Richard said with a smile. He sorted through the stacks of letters and photos on the table and turned to Lesley. "I don't see yours here. Are you telling me that you aren't going to submit your bio and half-naked photo for my consideration?"

Lesley sniffed in disdain as she studied her sandwich. "I'd rather spend a month searching the woods for coral snakes."

He laughed loudly. "Ah, Lesley. What a joker you are." He laid a hand on her arm and gave it a squeeze. "You're the kid sister I never had."

She pulled her arm away sharply. About to say something suitably witty in return, she heard the sound of the front doorbell and jumped up. "I'll get it. I could use the break."

Her linen napkin hit the table with a gentle plop as she hurried down the hall to open the large oak front door. A pretty blond woman in a lemon-colored dress stood smiling on the step.

"Hello," she said easily. "I'm Shawna. Is Richard here?"

Lesley felt herself staring and forced herself to snap to.

"Oh, I'm sorry. Yes, he is. Please come in." She stood back and the girl entered the foyer, the heavy scent of her perfume following her in. Lesley immediately recognized it as one of the more sensual perfumes that came packaged in a fiery red container. And even though she knew nothing about this girl, Lesley felt that the scent suited her. Tall, blond and cute in a feline way, she looked the sort of woman who could change from pussycat to tiger within minutes.

"I'll get— Oh, here he is now," Lesley said, motioning to Richard who was at that moment walking down the hall toward them. "Richard, this is Shawna. Shawna, this is—"

"*The* Richard Conway. I know," the girl said smoothly. She held out a perfectly manicured hand. "I'd recognize you anywhere."

Richard seemed immediately taken with their new guest and smiled in return. "I'm sorry, Shawna, but your name doesn't ring a bell. Have we met?"

"No, we haven't. I saw your picture in the magazine, *Northern Man Monthly,* and thought, well..." Her girlish giggle made Lesley's stomach curl. "I thought I'd be a little more aggressive than the others and look you up rather than send a letter. I mean, I find it a bit difficult to describe myself in words." She tossed her long blond hair over her shoulder and smiled expectantly.

It was all Lesley could do not to guffaw at the girl's transparency. Richard, however, was another case, and laid a guiding hand along the girl's waist.

"I know what you mean," he said kindly, showing her to one of the dark green sofas in the formal living room. "Lesley here was the one who wrote my biography and made me sound so wonderful. I have a lot to thank her for."

Uninvited but inexplicably drawn, Lesley found herself following them into the living room. She sat on the sofa opposite Richard and Shawna, her brow furrowing as she sat back and watched the scene unfold before her.

"If you wrote that article on Richard, then you're very talented," Shawna said with a quick glance over to Lesley. "You made him sound too good to resist."

"Don't feel you have to, then," he teased, and they both laughed.

Lesley stifled a groan, hiding it under a gentle cough. These two were not to be believed. Richard just wasn't like this, she thought tersely. He was bossy and arrogant and self-centered and lovable and funny and—

Lesley bit the inside of her lip until it hurt. That kind of thinking was going to get her nowhere. After all, it had been her own stupid idea to put Richard's ad in the magazine, not his. Mae had tried to warn her before the article went to the printer's, but had she listened? Oooh, no. She'd known exactly what she was doing.

As Lesley was about to stand up and excuse herself, Mae entered the room. Shifting in her seat, Lesley settled back, preparing to watch the woman put Shawna through her paces. But Mae was exceptionally cordial and appeared to be enjoying herself more than usual as she chatted about her magazine over coffee to a witty and pleasant Shawna.

Lesley became even more reclusive and said little for the rest of the time Shawna was their guest. Her only bright spot had been when Wolf barged into the room with his usual vitality. Lesley waited for Shawna to start shrieking over his wet nose on her hand, claim damages for the muddy paw prints on her light linen dress or cry over the broken nail she received when the dog insisted on shaking hands, but none of it happened. To Lesley's irritation, Shawna simply laughed off Wolf's actions and launched into a story of how she'd been raised in the country on a farm where her family bred big white Samoyeds.

Lesley finally could stand no more and left the room with a polite goodbye. She'd come to the conclusion that Shawna, who was now completely relaxed and chatting as easily as a long-lost friend, was just as nice as she seemed.

An upsetting thought at best, since if she thought that Shawna was nice, then Richard probably would think so, too. And if he thought that Shawna was nice, he'd probably find a dozen more honest and caring women just like her waiting in the wings for an audition as his wife.

Lesley forced back a sudden wave of frustrated tears and took a walk out to the barn, slipping carrots to the horses and hiding away in an empty stall. Leaning back in a bed of straw, she cursed the impetuosity that had made her suggest Richard for the cover of *Northern Man*. If she hadn't, maybe they would have beaten the odds and seen their fledgling relationship grow into something beautiful and special.

But not now. Not now that she'd given him half of the country's eligible women to choose from. Boy! Had she blown it this time.

Reluctantly, she left the solitude of the barn and returned to the big white house, entering by the back door. Richard was back at the kitchen table, earnestly poring over his photos, while Mae stood at the counter preparing a fresh red salmon for supper.

"Did Bambi finally leave?" Lesley asked, pouring herself a glass of orange juice and sitting down.

"Bambi?" Richard echoed. "No, it was Shawna who was just here. This," he said, pulling a snapshot of a doe-eyed brunette from a pile of brown-haired women, "is Bambi."

Lesley took the picture from him and turned it over. The words, *Bambi goes all the way for a Buck...* were written in delicate scrollwork with three hearts in lieu of ellipses.

"I don't believe these women," she said, tossing the picture down in disgust. "Is this a typical letter?"

"What's wrong with it?" Richard took the picture and scanned the girl's bikini-clad body. "Can't you take a joke?"

Lesley couldn't keep the anger out of her voice. "I can take a joke, all right, but this..." she said with a wave to the assorted piles, "this isn't funny."

"I agree. It's very serious." He sighed thoughtfully. "In fact, I think I may need help to keep everything in order. I don't suppose you'd consider helping me out?" he asked. "Maybe start a mini filing system. Categorize them by hair color, or state, or name, maybe. What do you think?"

Lesley looked at him in awe. "I think you're crazy, that's what I think. You actually want me," she said, pointing to herself, "to help *you* keep track of your women?" She huffed, shook her head, then huffed again.

"Is that a no?"

From somewhere in the background, Lesley registered Mae's muffled laughter. Before her sat the man she loved, surrounded with enough names and phone numbers to keep him dating for two lifetimes. Her heart was breaking, her nerves were as taut as violin strings and on top of it all, he wanted her to keep track of the women of his dreams!

She pulled herself up, raised an eyebrow and summoned her best look of disdain.

"I'd rather eat my own cooking for a month," she said coolly, then turned and left the kitchen to the sound of Richard's and Mae's deep and hearty laughter.

Chapter Eight

Richard waited for Lesley to storm into the cabin, then slammed the door shut behind them. "Well, it's not *my* fault that you're such a klutz!"

Lesley bristled at Richard's words and sent him a black glare. "Well, you could have *told* me it was slippery."

"What did you expect? It's a *river*. Besides, I told you not to go near the edge."

"Oh, sure. Right after I fell in."

"Women!" he retorted, dragging his boots and heavy, wet socks off. "You're all alike. Absolute—"

"Don't say it, Bucky. For your information, I happen to be very agile."

He scanned her body. "And that's why you're soaking wet?"

She sneered, grabbing her favorite plaid blanket from the chair and wrapping it about her body. She'd begun to chill on the way back from the creek but had been too proud to admit it. Now, though, the cold was beginning to make her visibly shiver.

"You need a hot bath," Richard said firmly, putting two big pans of water on the hot plate. "Get those clothes off. Right now."

Lesley felt like arguing and would have, had she not been shaking like a leaf.

"Am I going to catch some obnoxious disease now that I've fallen in a creek?" she demanded, wrestling her body and blanket to the bedroom door.

"Not unless you drank any of the water."

She hadn't, luckily being able to keep her mouth closed and her head above the waterline when she'd hit the rocky bottom of the shallow creek they'd hiked to earlier that afternoon. Things had been going so well, too, she mused, entering the bedroom and stripping from her wet clothes.

Although another five days of cards and letters had arrived since Shawna's unexpected visit, no other woman, save the one who had prompted their unscheduled visit to the cabin this afternoon, had shown up at the door looking for Richard. Lesley took that as a good sign, although she couldn't say how many letters Richard had answered. He seemed to be making a big deal of perusing the responses without actually sitting down and writing to any of the hopefuls.

It made her wonder if he'd found anyone suitable yet, or if he was waiting another week to see what the mail brought.

Shivering, Lesley wrapped her nakedness in Richard's duvet and lay down to wait for her bath. What more could a woman have to offer? she thought, questioning Richard's restraint. He'd been deluged with women over the past days, from doctors to waitresses, nurses to artists. Even a young pilot who flew her own small plane down in Florida. Surely she'd be the perfect woman for Richard. What was she missing? Lesley wondered.

What in heaven's name are you holding out for, Richard?

It was the same recurring conversation Lesley had had with herself every day for the past week. She'd given it so much thought, in fact, that she'd begun to get headaches. She decided to abandon the topic for a moment, and nestled deeper into Richard's bed, the scent of him on his pillow instantly filling her with need. Although they'd enjoyed a delicate truce this past week, she wanted the old camaraderie back. She wanted the closeness they'd shared before the article hit the newsstands. The touching. The kisses...

She didn't know how long she'd been lying there, either daydreaming or dozing, when the sound of Richard's voice pierced her thoughts.

"Ready!" he called, banging on the bedroom door.

Lesley jumped up, pulled the blanket tight around her and went into the living room. There, in the middle of the floor on a plastic mat, sat a round tin bathtub half filled with water. An interested Wolf sat watch over it, and a towel and the dish-washing detergent sat on the floor beside him.

She surveyed the items doubtfully. "That's it?"

"'Fraid so," he said, pouring in a huge pan of boiling water. "There. That's the best bath that tub has ever seen."

She looked into it. It did look inviting at that. As a matter of fact, considering how grungy she felt, with her skin covered in swamp water and her hair in knots, it looked darned inviting.

"Sorry there's no real shampoo," he said, waving to the detergent. "But that's just as good, maybe better." He tossed the bar of lye soap from the kitchen sink onto the pile of towels. "There, I think that should do it."

"What do you usually do when you want a bath?" she asked, testing the water with her toe.

"I go to the big house."

"Then why didn't you take me there?" she asked indignantly.

"Because you were cold and wet, and I didn't want you dripping on the upholstery of my truck. Besides, I was afraid Hortense might still be there—"

"Hazel," Lesley corrected.

"Whatever. Like I said, she might still have been there, waiting to jump my bones."

"So?"

"So?" he snapped. "Didn't you *see* what she was wearing?"

Lesley shrugged. "Lots of women wear black leather jackets."

"With a skull and crossbones burned into it?" He shook his head. "Oh, no. There was *no* way I was going—"

"Okay, fine. I see your point," Lesley argued. "But did you have to tell her that we were *engaged?*"

"You bet. Didn't you see her bike? She had a tent and a propane stove strapped to it! If I hadn't said I was spoken for, she might've pitched her tent and waited for me to get back."

"Don't flatter yourself," Lesley scoffed, testing the water with her big toe again. It was perfect. Any longer and it would be too cool to use. "Just remember that we're paid up. I don't owe you any more favors in return for putting your ad in *Northern Man*. No more cups of coffee prepared with ju-u-st the right amount of cream, no more mucking out the barn because you're beat from answering perfumed letters and no more helping with your filing system. Now get lost and let me take my bath.''

"Gladly," Richard grumbled. "C'mon, Wolf. We're not wanted here."

"No! Wolf stays with me. For protection."

"You're not going to want him here. It's—"

"It's my call, Bucky," she said firmly. "And I say he stays."

Richard looked at the dog, was about to say something, then shrugged. "Okay, but you'll be sorry."

She sneered as he left the cabin, and turned to Wolf. "Men!" she said, allowing the duvet to drop. She eased herself into the tin bath, which was surprisingly comfortable, and set about washing her hair. The detergent was lemon scented, and surprisingly effective in getting the grunge from her hair. As she rinsed, Wolf began to act skittish, whining and pacing back and forth as he sniffed at the bathwater.

"Wolf, behave yourself," Lesley chided. She laughed at the dog's antics, then ignored him while she scrubbed the clingy film from her skin. The feel of clean water rejuvenated her, making her feel human again. Wolf continued to bounce around her, yelping and whining, both ends of his body moving in different directions and his tail wagging wildly as he jumped about the tub.

"What's your problem?" Lesley teased. "Here, maybe this will cool you off," she added, splashing Wolf with a handful of soapy water.

That was all it took. Immediately the dog jumped into the tub, barking loudly and licking Lesley's face as he bounced up and down in the water. She screamed, long and loud, vainly fighting off Wolf's playful antics with her hands. Seconds later, the cabin door swung open, the dog's weight was gone and Richard's hand was dragging her upward.

"Down, Wolf," he commanded, his grin softening his words.

Lesley then stood before him, hair plastered to her face, her features drawn in an angry frown.

"That dog's crazy!" she shouted, pointing to the animal. Richard began to laugh and she felt her frown darken. "What are you laughing at?" she snarled, cursing all the Fates that had worked together to bring her to this time and place.

"You look rather, uh..." Richard shrugged and began laughing again.

A fierce red heat suffused Lesley's cheeks as realization dawned. She was naked as the day she was born, standing in a tub of water in the middle of a backwoods cabin, angrily denouncing the antics of a wolf-dog to a man who drove her crazy.

The absurdity of the situation brought frustrated tears to her eyes, and she grabbed an oversize bath towel from the floor and wrapped it around her dripping body.

"What was that damned dog thinking of, anyway?" she demanded, allowing Richard to help her from the tub. She snatched her arm away and pushed the hair from her eyes.

"It's his tub. I guess he wanted to get in on the act. You must have splashed him to make him jump inside."

"You gave me the *dog's* bathtub?"

"There isn't another one, and I didn't think you fit in the soup pot."

He began laughing again, sending Lesley's temper through the roof. Between Wolf's raucous barking and Richard's laughter, she wasn't sure he could hear her.

"It's not funny," she shouted.

"It is from where I'm standing," he insisted, waving Wolf down. But the dog would not be quietened and continued his excited, noisy barking.

"I can't believe this is happening to me," Lesley cried, pointing to the door "Both of you, *out!*"

In his hurry to oblige, Richard took several steps back with his hands raised in mock-surrender while Wolf continued to bounce around on all fours.

"Hey, no problem," Richard assured her, grabbing a gnarled twig from the woodpile. "We'll go do some whittling." But as he stood up, he caught his boot on the curled edge of the rug and had to grab for the chair to save himself. In doing so, he ground the rough end of the twig into his palm.

"Oh, no," Lesley cried, coming to his side. She grabbed his hand and looked at it. "Oh, Richard," she said, scanning his face. "You're bleeding." She took a stranglehold on his arm and eased him down into the chair while simultaneously trying to keep her towel tucked around her body. "Here, sit down. I'll get a towel."

"I'll be fine if you just stay away from me," he muttered. He looked at his hand and cursed the copious blood. "Has anyone ever told you that you're a walking disaster, Toots?"

She ignored his words and knelt down before him with a paper towel and the kettle of water.

"Shut up and let me see it," she argued, gently taking his hand. She dabbed at the cut, watching as he winced. "It's not that bad. I don't think you'll need stitches."

"Of course I won't. I'll be fine if you just give me the damned towel." He snatched it from her hand and held it to his palm. "You could get a bandage from the cupboard over the sink."

She did so, and unwrapped it.

"Take it easy, woman," he said, gingerly holding out his hand. She placed the bandage on the cut and sat back.

"I really am sorry," she said sincerely. "Do you think we should go back to the house?"

"What for?" He eased back in the soft armchair. "This is what country living is all about. It's a scratch. It'll be gone in a day." His look hardened. "It's a stupid accident that *we* think nothing of, but that could..."

His voice drifted away. Lesley knew the direction of his thoughts. As silly and negligible as the cut was, if it had happened to Richard's father and he'd ignored it in his usual carefree way, it could have had serious implications. So, too, her fall in the creek. Whereas she'd simply gotten up with her body intact but her pride hurt, he could have scratched himself on the rocks and started an infection that had the potential to threaten his life. Was it nagging thoughts like these that plagued Richard daily? That some insignificant little accident was going to lead, through neglect, to his father's death? If so, it was a heavy burden he bore.

And he was right. Even though Bob was relatively fit and competent, he still needed someone living at the house with him full-time, if only to monitor his comings and goings. She'd have to see if there was anything she could do to help arrange it before she left.

She looked at Richard and the dark hair that insisted on drooping onto his forehead, and felt a rush of need mixed with fear flood her body. She'd told herself not long ago that falling out of love with Richard was going to be just as easy as falling in love had been. But in looking at him now, she doubted that very much. If anything serious happened to this man... She shuddered at the thought.

Rising quietly, she went to the bedroom where she pulled on a sweatshirt and matching drawstring pants taken from Richard's bureau. Returning to the living room, she noticed that he'd fallen asleep on the chair, so she quietly cleaned up the mess caused by her fateful bath, putting everything except the tub back in its place. That she would have to leave for later, when Richard could help her drag it outside.

Lesley sat on the sofa and curled her feet beneath her, content to watch Richard's profile as he slept. He really was an attractive man, she mused, not surprised that he'd been deluged with letters and cards since his article had hit the magazine stands. She wondered which applicant he'd finally settle on, and immediately felt a sharp, jealous pang toward the nameless woman.

Sleepy innocence bathed his dormant features, softening his profile and making him appear harmless. Lesley grinned. He might be physically harmless, but he was wreaking havoc with her emotional well-being. As she watched, he stirred, flexed his jaw and opened his eyes. Scanning the room, his gaze settled on her and a smile flickered across his lips.

"Sorry. I must have dozed off." He stretched and gave a noisy yawn. "I was up late last night and early this morning."

"Why didn't you say something? We didn't have to come out today. Besides being tired, I bet you had a million things to do before leaving for Los Angeles tomorrow."

Richard smiled at Lesley's perceptiveness. "Yeah, I did, as a matter of fact. But nothing that couldn't wait." He dabbed at his hand. "Besides," he said, as he rose and took a seat next to her on the sofa, "I was just thinking the other day how I needed a scar on my hand." He laid an arm along the back of the sofa, close to but not touching Lesley's shoulder.

"I am sorry about your little accident. I want you to know that I'm really a very calm and rational person."

"Except around men?"

"Certain men, I guess. Men who bug me more than usual."

"Your boyfriend back in San Francisco must really have pushed you to the limit to get you as angry as he did." A pregnant pause. "Not that it's any of my business, but are you going back to him?"

She gave a mirthless laugh. "Not a chance."

"Because he didn't want you to have a career?"

"Among other things."

He wondered what those other things were. "How important is your career to you?" he asked instead.

"Very important," she answered immediately. "I spent too many years in a job I hated, to give it up now. Besides, I'm just starting. It's still really new and exciting to me." She plucked at the sweatshirt she wore. "I might feel different in a few years, but for now, I'm in for the long haul."

That's what I was afraid of.

"That's great," he said, and meant it. Just because her plans were destined to take her away from him didn't mean he wasn't happy to see her follow her dream. Everyone needed dreams, even if they were, like his, impossible to achieve.

He really had no right feeling sorry for himself, he thought abruptly. After all, he'd been the one to suddenly pull back from this relationship, not Lesley. She'd kissed him like the devil earlier that day, showing him in no uncertain terms that she was interested in him.

"What about marriage?" he asked, needing to know. "How would you manage something like that?"

She pursed her lips. "I don't know. I've never given it much thought, so I'm not sure how I'd go about it. I'd still want to work. And I love traveling, so I'd want to keep doing that, too. I guess it will have to be something I work out when the time comes."

Richard rubbed a finger along the faded knee of his jeans. "Traveling can be fun," he admitted. "But it can also be lonely. It's nice to come home after a trip. To things and people you know. To your own kitchen, your own bedroom."

To your wife and kids.

Richard imagined himself coming home after a long trip such as the one he'd been on this past week, to find Lesley waiting for him. The thought stirred him, but he forced it back. There was no way that was ever going to happen. Not now that he was making plans to base out of Alaska and spend his days flying back and forth to California.

Richard sighed and rubbed the back of his aching neck. Just thinking about the nomadic turn his life was about to take made his head hurt. He was too old and too tired to be flying around the country like some cocksure kid straight out of school. He wanted a more normal life, one where predictability and routine figured highly.

"A penny for your thoughts," Lesley said.

He looked into her eyes and knew that if he lived to be a hundred, he'd remember their exact shade of blue.

"Do you believe in fate?" he asked suddenly.

She seemed visibly taken aback by his question. "I guess so. At least I believe that fate gives us choices. Whether we take one road or another, well, that's up to us."

He considered her words. Was that what had happened here? Had he been given two choices? Force his father to move to accommodate his own preferences, or change his life-style and give up the things that mattered to him, such as one mailing address, to accommodate his father?

"But what if you make the wrong decision?" he asked.

Lesley's hand came out and rested on his. "If, after thinking both sides through, you decide to choose one road over the other, know in your heart that it was the only choice you could make."

Richard nodded, knowing that choosing his father's well-being over his own happiness had been the right thing to do. It was just too damn bad that the only real choice was the one that had demanded that he give up the woman he loved. At least he'd be able to sleep nights, knowing that both Lesley and his father had been given what they'd been fighting for: the survival of Conway House and his father's right to live there.

Richard turned to Lesley.

"You're very wise, do you know that, Miss Lyndstrom? Very wise, and painfully beautiful."

"Painfully?" she said with a little laugh. "And just where does my beauty hurt you?"

Richard lifted her hand to his heart, firmly pressing her palm against his chest.

"Right here," he murmured.

Lesley caught her breath. Her own heart was beating a tattoo against her rib cage, filling her with its own brand of pain. The long-denied pain of wanting.

"Maybe I should kiss it and make it better," she whispered back.

"Maybe you should."

She hesitated slightly, the heat in her veins telling her to proceed with caution. But her own heart told her that there was no safe way of handling this situation, so she raised her somewhat shaky hands and loosened first one, then another of Richard's shirt buttons. He didn't try to stop her, merely held her gaze as her fingers continued their mission. When the third button came loose, Lesley smoothed back the fabric of his shirt and exposed Richard's chest to her greedy eyes.

If he was breathing, he was doing so with great control. She, in comparison, was breathing so erratically that it was questionable if she'd be able to continue her exploration. She'd known that Richard's body was a beautiful sight to behold, but that knowledge was nothing when compared to the way it felt beneath her palms. He was a magnificent male, warm and firm, and smelled like musk mixed with outdoors.

Lesley licked her lips, preparing them for contact with his body, then leaned forward and with a feather touch, kissed that muscular part of his chest that housed his heart. He stiffened at the contact and leaned back into the corner of the sofa, his hands around her upper arms pulling her with him until she lay by his side.

Bracing herself on one elbow, she allowed her other hand free rein. The muscles of Richard's chest were hard from a life of physical work, the skin taut and golden from the sun. She stroked the ripples of his torso, irritated when his shirt got in her way. As slowly as her greedy emotions would allow, she pulled the shirt from his waistband and laid his body open to her hungry gaze.

"Does it still hurt?" she asked, tilting her face toward him.

"A little," he answered, his jaw tightening.

She nodded, and returned her gaze to his chest. Again she licked her lips. "Let's see what we can do about that, then."

Leaning forward, Lesley ran her tongue over Richard's flat nipple. He sucked in a deep, shuddering breath, telling her without words how her touch affected him. She nurtured the other one with the same care and attention, gently suckling it until Richard suddenly reached out and ran a tense hand through her hair, stilling her.

"Lesley." A deep, shuddering sigh. "Do you know what you're doing?"

She lifted her head and smiled sensuously. Richard's thigh beneath her palm felt tense and hard. "I'm making it better."

"No!" he said sharply, reaching out his other hand and pulling her toward him.

He seemed angry or frustrated, or both, and Lesley didn't understand.

"You're making it hurt *more*," he ground out, taking her mouth in a hard, demanding kiss. His hand at the back of her neck held her still, while his other ran the length of her.

He drew every last drop of emotion from her willing body, drinking it like a dying man in need of water. His grip tightened, almost painfully, and when he pulled away and looked deep into her eyes, Lesley knew she was losing him.

"Richard, I don't understand—"

"We shouldn't do this, Lesley. You know that, don't you?"

"No, I don't know that. I only know that what we have is special. And frightening. I'm losing control of my life, Richard, and I don't seem to care anymore." She ran a hand along his bare chest, but he laid a palm over it and stopped its journey. "I don't want anything to ruin this night," she said earnestly. "I want it to last forever."

Forever.

That one word, simply spoken, brought Richard back down to earth with a sickening thud. He swallowed hard, knowing he had been forced to choose one of those roads that Lesley had spoken of, and gently pushed her away.

"I don't think we'd better let this go any further," he said brusquely. "It would be a mistake."

He tried to make his voice sound comforting, but it emerged a tortured growl. Lesley pulled back quickly, pain and confusion clouding her normally pretty features.

"You're right, of course," she said vaguely. She ran a hand over her cheek. "I'm embarrassed. I'm not usually so dense."

He ached to pull her close, but didn't dare in case he ignited the passion between them.

"I'm the one who should be embarrassed, Lesley," he said, easing away from her. "I'm not some teenager in the back of my dad's car. There are too many reasons why I shouldn't have let this get out of hand." He squeezed his eyes shut for a moment. "God help me, but I just don't have any willpower where you're concerned."

She shook her head and ran a hand through her hair several times, looking anywhere but at him. She was trying to appear nonchalant and in control, but Richard knew her well enough to know that she was dying a thousand deaths, the same as he. He stood and tried to adjust his jeans without being too obvious.

"I'm sorry," he said abruptly, doing up the buttons on his shirt. "Did you want anything to eat before heading back?"

She rose as well. "No, thanks." She hiked up the sweat suit pants that were too big for her frame. "I'd just as soon get going, if that's all right with you."

"Sure. You stay here. I'll empty the bath and get the horses ready."

Dragging the tub behind him, he immediately left the cabin, not trusting himself to keep his distance from Lesley. Every instinct screamed at him to take her in his arms and show her how much he cared, while every modicum of common sense told him that doing such a thing would only make matters worse.

When he approached the horses five minutes later, Caesar gave him a sharp nudge to the shoulder, as though pushing him back toward the cabin.

"Sorry, my friend," he told the animal. "I'm afraid that's a road I'm not free to take."

Another glimpse to the cabin and the feminine frame outlined in the hazy interior, and Richard turned back to the horses, his heart that of a tormented man.

Chapter Nine

It was the last week of August. The crisp, cool scent of fall filled the air. Lesley stood at the end of the long, wooden dock, reveling in the contrast of white-capped mountain against placid lake as a slight morning breeze ruffled her loose hair. Dawn had broken quiet and serene, slightly overcast on this, her third, and last, day at the fly-in fishing camp belonging to one of Richard's close friends.

She'd been quick to accept the offer of a weekend away, as had Bob and Mae, in celebration of another successful season at Conway House. The guests were gone now, and the boardinghouse lay empty as it would until the following spring. Richard was due back in California in a week and although he hadn't said anything, Lesley sensed that he'd made plans of some sort with regard to his father.

The two men had disappeared several times these past days, saying they were going fishing but more

often than not returning empty-handed. Lesley had a
strong feeling they'd been off somewhere talking,
perhaps working out an as-yet-unveiled plan regarding Bob, Conway House and the future of both.

Lesley cast a look at the floatplane anchored to the
dock and sighed. Not only was her trip to the fishing
camp coming to an end, so, too, was her time at Conway House. She gazed across the cool mirrored sur-
face of the lake, valiantly trying to absorb its beauty
to relive another day. A red-breasted merganser slid
across Lesley's line of vision, leaving a trail of ripples
in its wake. Only the gentle swaying of the trees along
the shoreline and the water lapping against the dock
marred the silence. Beauty surrounded Lesley, enveloping her like the pink cloak of sunset that tinted the
mountain at day's end. Nature reigned supreme. All
was right with the world....

And then she heard Mae.

"Bucky, don't you tell me I can't take this hamper.
If it doesn't go, *I* don't go."

Lesley smiled ruefully, knowing her time alone with
nature had come to an end, and turned to the foot of
the dock. Richard, clad in his usual jeans and leather
aviator jacket, was walking toward her, carrying what
looked to be a bag of mail, while Mae, dressed in a
garish purple jumpsuit and matching chiffon scarf
struggled beside him with a wicker hamper.

"And I'm telling you, Maesy," he said, grabbing
one of the handles to help her, "I'd just as soon take
your hamper and leave you behind."

Lesley didn't catch Mae's sharp retort, probably just
as well since the woman had a repertoire to make a
sailor blush. Richard, however, seemed impervious to
her words and approached Lesley with a broad grin.

"So this is where you got to," he said, easing his end of the hamper to the dock. He stretched and rubbed his shoulder. "I'm sending you my doctor's bill," he said, pointing to Mae.

"Pansy."

"Troublemaker," he answered, opening the plane's side door. Lesley began to laugh. "Don't encourage her, Toots," Richard warned. "You know how she gets."

Lesley watched as he tossed the bag of mail into the hold and hoisted himself in after it. He was an agile man, in better shape than many men ten years his junior, with broad shoulders, long muscular legs and a lazy grace that she found intoxicating. No matter how often she found herself around him, or how much time they spent talking, she never tired of his company. As far as she was concerned, if she spent the rest of her life with Richard, it wouldn't be long enough.

A familiar ache pierced her heart, erasing the smile from her face and warning that her thoughts were straying into dangerous waters. She took a deep breath, smiled brightly and grabbed one of the suitcases sitting on the dock.

"Are we ready to go?" she asked, swinging it up to Richard.

"Yep," he said, taking a second suitcase and a duffle bag from her. He tucked them away into a corner, but already the plane was filling up. "Dad should be along any minute."

"When do you want me in the plane?" Mae asked, arms akimbo. "I'm sitting up front with you this time. You might need help navigating."

Richard guffawed. "Maesy, you couldn't navigate your way out of a paper bag." He heaved another duffle bag into the plane. "Nope, you're sitting right where you belong. In the back with your hamper," he added, winking broadly at Lesley.

Lesley laughed at their irreverence, a thin veneer that did little to hide a deep and warm friendship, and felt another stab of regret that her time with these people was quickly coming to an end. Another week putting Conway House back together and Lesley would have no reason to stay on. Mae was due to return to her newly redecorated house in three days while Richard had his plane ticket for Los Angeles and was leaving in five days. Lesley still didn't know if Bob would be accompanying him back, and since their plans didn't concern her, wouldn't ask.

Maybe when they got back to Conway House today, she'd tell them about the plans she'd made regarding her own future. She hadn't told anyone, not even Mae, about the offer of a junior position on the local newspaper, or the success she'd had selling her stories on Alaska to the newspaper back in San Francisco. They'd loved the two she'd already sent down and had even given her a contact with a travel magazine who was always, according to the editor, looking for well-researched, well-written articles.

She had, Lesley thought, attained a modest success in a very short time and was now optimistic that she'd be able to support herself doing what she loved most. With her career settled, now all she had to do was find a place to stay. Although Conway House would have suited her fine, she'd already told Richard that she'd be moved out by the beginning of September, knowing that she stood, unfairly, in the way of his plans. Whatever Richard had worked out with his father was

his business, and he'd implement it without her inter-
ference.

It was the least she could do for the man she loved
after causing him so much aggravation this summer.
Lesley looked over to the object of her affection and
realized that he was still arguing with Mae over the
hamper.

"Well, don't blame me if we go down because I'm
overloaded," he griped, hauling the hamper on to the
plane from a wheezing Mae.

Lesley snapped to, and helped push the heavy wicker
box on board. Richard had no sooner tucked it away
behind her seat than Wolf came bounding down the
dock and jumped in beside it. Bob hurried along behind. He looked happy, fit and rested, as though he
could take on the world without missing a step. What
he'd lost in excess weight during Mae's stay at the
house, he'd gained tenfold in energy and enthusiasm.
In fact, he got along so well with Mae that it was now
difficult to imagine one without the other.

"Ready, Rich?" Bob asked, hiking up jeans that
now needed suspenders to stay afloat. "You got everything?"

"I'll say," Richard answered, slipping from the
plane. "I got a damned hernia." Ignoring Mae's
blustering, he tossed out several comments of his own
regarding overbearing passengers and weight restric-
tions on small aircraft, then jumped onto the dock as
Bob settled in after Mae.

"Ready, Toots?" Richard asked, coming over to
her. "Lesley," he added quietly. "Are you all right?"

She smiled and nodded, hoping to hide the tears
that were close to spilling down her cheeks, then

wrapped her arms about her as she took one last look at the mountains and lake.

"I'm fine," she said softly. "I just...just..."

Warm hands came to cup her shoulders as Richard pulled her back into his embrace. "What is it? Tell me," he whispered in her ear.

She weakened, loving the feel and scent of him, needing him by her side always while knowing it was destined not to be.

"I—I love it here," she stammered, bracing her shoulders. Richard's hands stroked her arms, then loosely clasped her waist, drawing her to his warmth and the scent of leather mixed with musk. "I don't want it to end."

"The trip to the fishing camp?"

"Everything." She sighed. "I want everything to stay just the way it is, forever."

Several moments passed. "You know that's impossible, don't you?" he asked gently.

Lesley's breath caught in her throat. "Yes," she whispered. "Yes, I do." She squeezed her eyes shut and took a deep, shaky breath. "I know it's time to move on. I just had such a good time this summer that I'm afraid of never being this happy again."

Richard tightened his hold. "You will be. Trust me," he told her, turning her in his arms. He looked down into her eyes and smiled confidently. "Trust me."

Lesley's eyes had drifted closed long before Richard's lips met hers. She opened to him, accepting his kiss with longing and love, sliding her palms beneath his jacket and along his back as his tongue slipped inside her mouth and met hers. Passion quickly took control, tossing out common sense and raging through Lesley like a northern bonfire.

She belonged to this man. She wanted to belong to this man. And, surprisingly enough, she wasn't afraid of losing herself in him. In fact, she welcomed it....

"You two lovebirds gonna play kissy face all day?" Mae called from the open plane door. "Or are we going to get this show on the road?"

Lesley jerked back and felt a hot blush flood her cheeks. She stifled a nervous laugh and brushed a hand over her khaki walking shorts. Richard, who stood with his back to the plane, glanced to the heavens and grinned wryly.

"Have you ever, Toots, known anyone with such bad timing?"

Lesley laughed shakily. "Can't say I have." She took another step back. "Although I guess we should get going."

Concern shadowed Richard's face as he cupped her cheek with his palm. "Are you all right?"

"Sure, sure," she said with a wave of her hand. "Like the lady says, let's get this show on the road."

Richard hesitated, staring deep into her eyes before nodding and helping her into the plane. Seconds later she was sitting up front, strapping herself in as he took his seat beside her.

"Now, remember what I told you last time, Bucky," Mae piped up from the back. "Take it nice and slow. You know how bumpy rides give me indigestion."

"No, I didn't know," Richard said, flashing a wicked smile Lesley's way. He winked. "But thanks for telling me."

Within minutes they were airborne, skimming above the treetops on their way to Anchorage and Conway

House. Lesley sighed contentedly and nestled in to enjoy the ride until twenty minutes later when the weather took a turn for the worse.

"Are we flying into a storm?" she asked, noticing Richard's sudden concentration.

"Not really."

"What do you mean, not really?" Mae barked from the back.

"Yeah, Rich. You got everything under control?"

"Yes, Dad, I do." But even as he spoke, he was circling a small silver-gray lake protected by a ridge of thick, heavy evergreens.

Lesley felt a ripple of fear, which she quickly pushed aside. "Are we going down?" she asked quietly.

"Going down?" Mae echoed. "I don't like the sound of that."

"Have to, Maesy," Richard called out. "It's the hamper, you understand."

Lesley knew he was trying to make light of a tense situation and gave him the peace and quiet she knew he needed to safely land the plane. He did so, flawlessly, and cut the engine after stopping close to a narrow peninsula off the lake's edge.

"Why did we stop?" Mae immediately wanted to know.

"The weather." Richard pointed to the storm clouds scudding across the sky. "I'd rather see them pass than fly into them. If that's all right with you, of course."

"No problem, Rich," his father assured him. "Always better to be safe than sorry." A moment's hesitation. "So what we gonna do now?"

"Let's eat."

Richard and Lesley shared a smile over Mae's remark and felt the plane rock gently as she pulled the wicker hamper from behind her seat.

"Take it easy back there, woman," Richard warned. "You keep throwing your weight around, and we'll tip for sure." He twisted in his seat. "What have you got in that thing anyway?—oh, jeez."

Lesley shifted also and watched Mae pull a huge bottle of homemade wine from a cooler deep in the hamper. "Mae!" she said in surprise. "No wonder you wouldn't leave without it."

"Damned right. This stuff is good. *Real* good. No way was I leaving it behind." She grabbed a tall glass and filled it. "There you go, Lesley. Enjoy. Bucky, you get a cola because you're driving."

"Thanks," he said dryly. "What about those pastries?" he added, pointing to a box with a see-through window. "You're going to share them, aren't you?"

"I wasn't going to," Mae admitted. "But since you've seen them, I guess I'll have to."

"Can I have one, too?" Bob asked hopefully, as Richard took the biggest one from the box of ten.

Mae eyed him for a moment. "Sure. You watched what you ate back at the camp. Go ahead. Have one."

"How d'ya know I didn't eat a lot?" he asked, quickly biting into the sugary bun and sighing like a man on his way to heaven.

Lesley smiled. She, too, had noticed that Bob had been careful about what he ate, although whether that was because he cared about his health or feared Mae's wrath was hard to say.

"I've been watching you, of course." Mae munched on her own pastry. "There hasn't been a thing you've eaten in the past seven weeks that I didn't know about.''

"And that's the truth," Lesley whispered to Richard.

He nodded thoughtfully and recalled the conversations on health, competence and moving that he'd had with his father that weekend. Although Richard had decided weeks ago not to push the subject of selling Conway House, he'd needed to hear one last time that staying in Alaska was still paramount to the man. It was, and now Richard knew it was time to implement the plan to keep him in Conway House.

He took a long swig of his soft drink and forged full steam ahead. "So, Mae," he said, casually scanning his tin of cola, "you ready to go home?"

"You mean fly? Now?" She looked dubious. "I thought you said we were going to wait out the weather.''

"No, I don't mean fly. I mean home. Your home. Your house in Anchorage. Are you ready to go home?''

"Oh, that.'' She shrugged and grabbed another pastry after offering seconds to Lesley. "Sure. I guess so.''

"You don't sound very excited.''

"What's to get excited about? It's a house. Four walls. A whole lot of doors and a roof.''

Lesley watched Richard nod thoughtfully. He certainly was interested in the writing on his can of pop. Idly she wondered what was going on in that brain of his, because if she knew anything about the almighty Buck Conway, it was that he was up to something.

"Well," he said finally. "I guess it's about time I told you about my plan.''

"Aw, not another one, Rich," Bob complained. "I hate your plans. They always got me movin'."

Richard rubbed his palm along the knee of his jeans. Lesley recognized it as a sign that he was choosing his words carefully and sat back to watch the scene unfold.

"Well, Dad, you don't have to worry about that anymore." A pregnant pause. "Because I've decided to sell my company and move back into Conway House."

Dead silence descended. Outside, the wind buffeted the trees along the shoreline. A light rain tapped the windows of the plane. No one seemed to be breathing.

"Did you hear me?" he asked.

"I did, Bucky," Mae said sharply, "but I don't believe you."

He shrugged and guzzled the last of his pop. "Believe it. That's why I went back to California a couple of weeks ago. To set the wheels in motion."

Lesley's heart dropped. She knew Richard's company meant the world to him. Anyone who knew anything about him knew that. He'd built it from the ground up, taking a small initial investment and turning it into a prestigious, high-powered firm well respected in the field. Add to that the enormous expansion due to begin in just a few weeks, and it was simply unthinkable that he'd give it up.

"Richard, are you sure you want to do that?" Lesley asked with concern. "I mean, it's your company—"

"Yeah, Rich." His father butted in. "You thought this through yet?"

Mae snorted loudly. "Of course he hasn't. Any horse's rear would know that it's the stupidest idea he's ever come up with—"

"Whoa, everyone!" Richard held up a hand. "What the hell's going on here? This is what you've been bugging me for. What's the big deal? You're all getting what you wanted." He looked to Lesley, who was gripping her wineglass with clenched fingers. "You're the one who told me that Dad deserved to stay in his house." He looked back to his father. "And you're the one who refused to leave, saying it would kill you to give up the place." A final look to Mae. "And you're the one who helped put me on the cover of your damned magazine, all to keep me out of Dad's hair. So I finally realized," he continued, "that it was time I faced the fact that Dad needs me here."

"No, I don't. I don't need no baby-sitter lookin' after me. I'm doin' just fine on my own."

"No, you're not," Mae argued, swigging back her wine. "You need someone to look after you more than any man I know."

"Says who?"

"Says me."

"So what're you gonna do about it?"

"Well, Mr. I-don't-need-a-baby-sitter Conway, maybe I'll just stick around Conway House and make sure you don't sneak those extra cookies like you're always trying to."

When Richard sat back and smiled smugly, a light went on in Lesley's brain. She tilted her head, eyeing the confident way he was chuckling to himself, and knew that this was exactly where he'd steered the con-versation. She leaned forward so the two arguing adults in the back couldn't hear and toasted Richard with her wineglass.

"Nice going, Buck," she said, with a knowing smile of her own. "I haven't seen anything that smooth since my brother talked me into trading my allowance for a box of dirt." His grin widened. "You had no intention of selling your company, did you?"

"I would have, yes." His smile faded slightly. "Dad's well-being is important to me. I'd have done whatever it took to make sure he was taken care of."

She sipped her wine, some of the meanest rotgut she'd ever tasted, and eyed him. "Why not just *ask* Mae to stay on at Conway House?"

He shook his head. "Wouldn't have worked. I wanted her to offer to stay. When she didn't, I realized that she was probably afraid of being rejected." He sat back and sighed. "So I devised a plan to force her into action and make it look like staying was her idea. That way Dad couldn't accuse me of being, I believe the word is, *manipulative.*"

Lesley flushed and accepted his gibe. "Well, so now you've got your father taken care of, what's next? Another couple of days here and then back to California?"

"Yeah, I suppose so." Richard considered all that was going on back home and was surprised to find his mood one of disinterest. Now that the plans for the company expansion had been finalized and set in motion, he had little desire to be in on the day-to-day details. Especially now that he'd managed to land one of the top business executives in the country as his right-hand man to oversee the running of the company. It had been something he'd been trying to do for years— sign this executive to a long-term contract—but in doing so, Richard realized that he had just made himself obsolete.

The thought made him laugh out loud.

"What's so funny?" Lesley asked. She'd been watching when his gaze had drifted off, and wondered where his thoughts were taking him this time.

"Hmm? Oh, nothing," Richard answered, swigging down the last of his cola. "Just thinking about what I should do now."

"As in?"

He turned to her and smiled almost ruefully. "As in, with my life."

"Oh." Lesley swallowed hard. It wasn't the answer she'd been expecting. "What do you want to do with it?"

Richard shrugged. "It doesn't matter. It isn't possible."

"Anything's possible if you really want it."

He considered her words. "Think so?"

"I know so," she answered firmly. "I'm living proof that if you really want to do something in life, you should damn the consequences and just do it."

"Brave words."

She softened her tone and smiled shyly. "You know what I mean." She nestled back against the side of the plane and tilted her head. "What is it that you really want to do?"

He hesitated. "Get married."

"Married!" Lesley sat up straight in her seat, splashing her shorts with the wine in her glass.

"Yeah," he said, easing back in his seat and facing her. "I really want to get married."

Lesley's skin prickled. This was much worse than she'd thought. Buck, *married*. Her stomach turned.

He'd found someone through the magazine ad! Her stomach turned again. And it was all thanks to *her* that he'd found his dream woman.

Lesley downed the last of her wine and gripped the glass with ice-cold fingers. "Do you have someone special picked out?"

"Oh, yeah," he said meaningfully. "She's special, all right."

Lesley didn't dare meet Richard's eyes in case he read the utter despair in her gaze. "Oh. Well. I'm, uh...happy for you."

"Don't be. Like I said, it would never work out."

Her gaze darted to his face. Much as she hated the thought of Richard belonging to another woman, she hated the idea of him suffering unrequited love even more.

"Why wouldn't it work out?" she asked sharply.

Richard idly crushed the empty cola can in one hand and tutted thoughtfully. "She's got a career that's really important to her. I can't ask her to give that up."

"Why would she have to?"

"It involves a lot of traveling. Moving around, relocating, that sort of thing. Me, I want to stay in one place. Maybe raise a family."

"Oh." Lesley frowned at the vision of Richard's children with another woman. "Couldn't she base herself in one spot and travel from there?" she asked, forcing her thoughts to more neutral waters.

"I don't know."

"Then you should ask," Lesley insisted. Frustration filled her. It wasn't like Richard to be so passive. What the devil had got into him?

"I'm afraid to," he admitted. "She might think I'm being bossy, telling her how to run her life and all."

Lesley shook her head, a faint suspicion becoming more and more distinct. Richard hardly sounded afraid. In fact, he sounded almost teasing, as though he were pulling her leg. "Have you really found someone, or are you just joking?"

"No, no. I've found someone. She just doesn't like bossy men, that's all."

"What?" Lesley was trying to stay calm, but her heart was pounding out of her chest. "What do you mean, she doesn't like bossy men? What's that got to do with anything? I mean, did you ever try to run her life?"

"Not exactly."

"Did you ever try to get her to give up her career?"

"Never."

"Then why would she think you're bossy? Did she actually call you that?"

Richard frowned thoughtfully. "No," he drawled. "She didn't. It was more of a, 'That's right, Bucky. I put your ad in the magazine to find you a girlfriend and keep you out of my hair,' sort of thing."

Lesley was silenced by a mixture of confusion and happiness. But Mae had no such problem. Slapping her generous knee and peering around Lesley's seat, she said, "In case you don't get it, he's asking you to marry him."

Lesley was under a similar assumption, but not wanting to appear forward, she simply pointed to the unfinished bottle of wine on the floor by Mae's feet. "I think you'd better lay off that stuff, Mae—"

Bob poked his head into the aisle. "That right, Rich? You askin' Lesley, here, to get married?"

"Don't be ridiculous—" Lesley argued, embarrassment burning her cheeks.

"What I'm saying is that I'd like to, but I can't."

Lesley nearly dropped her glass. Her gaze immediately scanned Richard's face for some hint of a joke, but he was as serious as she'd ever seen him.

"Why can't you?" Mae demanded.

"Yeah, why can't you?" Lesley echoed breathlessly.

"Because of your career," he said solemnly.

"What about it?" she asked vacantly. She felt dizzy and light-headed, as though she'd fallen down a long tunnel after a white rabbit, and wondered if she was hallucinating.

"It's important to you."

"Uh-huh. So?"

He frowned slightly. "So, I can't ask you to give it up."

"Okay. I won't. So what's that got to do with getting married?"

"Yeah, Bucky," Mae piped up. "Make your point."

Richard scowled back at Mae then turned to Lesley, taking her glass and setting it on the floor. "Lesley, you have your whole career ahead of you. It's all you've talked about since coming to Alaska. I can't ask you to give that up now that you're ready to move on. Especially since I've made plans to move back here permanently and can't relocate."

Lesley's heart soared. "You're moving back to Alaska?"

"That's right. I've hired someone to take care of the San Francisco operation and plan to expand the Anchorage end of things. Maybe start a tour company specializing in fishing trips."

Lesley squeezed her eyes shut, too overcome with emotion to risk talking. When she opened them again seconds later, Richard was watching her with concern.

"Are you all right?" he asked, leaning toward her.

She nodded, her eyes brimming with tears. "Uh-huh. I'm just real happy."

"Happy?" he repeated. "Why?"

"Because I'm not going anywhere."

"You're not?"

She shook her head. "Nope," she said between deep breaths. "I'm staying in Anchorage."

"How?" Mae barked, poking her face forward.

Lesley wiped the tears from her eyes and laughed as she turned to the back of the plane. "I was offered a job on the newspaper last week. It's just a junior position," she added quickly, "but it's a foot in the door."

"Way to go, Les," Bob said brightly. "See, Rich. I told you she was made of stronger stuff."

"Yeah, you did," Richard smiled at Lesley. "Well, I guess this changes everything, doesn't it?"

She bit her lip, breathlessly waiting for him to speak.

"So ask her, for heaven's sake," Mae prodded.

Richard shrugged and grinned at Lesley. "I love you. So, you wanna get married?"

Lesley laughed out loud and listened to Mae whoop loudly from behind. "You bet she does!" she barked. "Bob, honey, get another glass out for Buck. This calls for a celebration!"

While the two fussed in the back for a suitable engagement feast, Richard pulled Lesley forward until she felt his warmth like a cloak.

"This wasn't the way I envisioned it," he admitted. He stroked her hair and ran a palm along her cheek. "I hope you're not disappointed that your proposal turned into a three-ring circus."

Lesley reached up and caressed the back of his hand with her own. "Disappointed? Are you kidding?" She drew his hand to her lips and gently kissed his palm. "Everything was just perfect."

He slid his hand along her neck and held her tight. "Are you sure marriage is going to fit in with your career?"

"Positive."

"What about a place to live?"

"How about Conway House?" she answered quickly.

"You wouldn't mind?"

She laughed lightly. "Not in the least." She leaned forward and stole a kiss. "In fact, I think life at Conway House could be good, Bucky." She kissed him soundly and slid her hands around his neck. "Yeah . . . *real* good!"

* * * * *

**HE'S MORE THAN
A MAN, HE'S
ONE OF OUR**

UNCLE DADDY

Kasey Michaels

Gabe Logan was doing just fine raising his orphaned niece alone. He didn't need or *want* any help from the baby's aunt, Erica Fletcher. Gabe could see that the uptight businesswoman didn't have a clue about child rearing. So when Erica suggested Gabe teach her about parenting, it was an offer he couldn't resist. Having her move into his house would surely force Erica to admit defeat. But when she set out to conquer his heart... Gabe knew he was in big trouble!

Find out the true meaning of *close quarters* in Kasey Michaels's UNCLE DADDY, available in February.

Fall in love with our **Fabulous Fathers**—and join the Silhouette Romance family!

FF293

**Three All-American beauties discover
love comes in all shapes and sizes!**

ALL-AMERICAN SWEETHEARTS

by Laurie Paige

CARA'S BELOVED (#917)—*February*

SALLY'S BEAU (#923)—*March*

VICTORIA'S CONQUEST (#933)—*April*

A lost love, a new love and a hidden one, three
All-American Sweethearts get their men in Paradise Falls,
West Virginia. Only in America...and only
from Silhouette Romance!

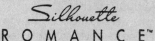

R O M A N C E™

SMYTHESHIRE, MASSACHUSETTS.

Small town. Big secrets.

**Silhouette Romance invites you to visit Elizabeth August's
small town, a place with a legacy rooted deep
in the past....**

THE VIRGIN WIFE
February 1993
Madaline MacGreggor-Smythe lived a far-from-ordinary existence. Though married, she had never experienced romantic intimacy and probably never would. But when Colin Darnell—a man from Madaline's past—returns to town, feelings long denied are rekindled. And so is the danger that had separated them!

HAUNTED HUSBAND
March 1993—FABULOUS FATHERS
Thatcher Brant, widower and father of two, vowed never to love again. This chief of police would not risk his feelings, or those of his children, for anyone. Least of all, Samantha Hogan. But *something* had told Samantha that Thatcher was the husband for her!

SMYTHESHIRE, MASSACHUSETTS—this sleepy little town has plenty to keep you up at night. Only from Silhouette Romance!

Silhouette
R O M A N C E™

SREA1

It takes a very special man to win

She's friend, wife, mother—she's you! And beside each Special Woman stands a wonderfully *special* man. It's a celebration of our heroines—and the men who become part of their lives.

Look for these exciting titles from Silhouette Special Edition:

January **BUILDING DREAMS** by Ginna Gray

February **HASTY WEDDING** by Debbie Macomber

March **THE AWAKENING** by Patricia Coughlin

April **FALLING FOR RACHEL** by Nora Roberts

Don't miss THAT SPECIAL WOMAN! each month—from your special authors.

AND

For the most special woman of all—you, our loyal reader—we have a wonderful gift: a beautiful journal to record all of your special moments. See this month's THAT SPECIAL WOMAN! title for details.

TSW1

Silhouette
ROMANCE™

HEARTLAND HOLIDAYS

Christmas bells turn into wedding bells for the Gallagher siblings in Stella Bagwell's *Heartland Holidays* trilogy.

THEIR FIRST THANKSGIVING (#903) in November
Olivia Westcott had once rejected Sam Gallagher's proposal—and in his stubborn pride, he'd refused to hear her reasons why. Now Olivia is back...and it is about time Sam Gallagher listened!

THE BEST CHRISTMAS EVER (#909) in December
Soldier Nick Gallagher had come home to be the best man at his brother's wedding—not to be a groom! But when he met single mother Allison Lee, he knew he'd found his bride.

NEW YEAR'S BABY (#915) in January
Kathleen Gallagher had given up on love and marriage until she came to the rescue of neighbor Ross Douglas...and the newborn baby he'd found on his doorstep!

Come celebrate the holidays with Silhouette Romance!